"The Vetala of Crystal Vellam Inlet" by Simo Srinivas first appeared in *Decoded Pride #3* (2022). "Mother Mansrot in the Glass Mountain" by Sarah Pauling first appeared in *Aseptic and Faintly Sadistic: An Anthology of Hysteria Fiction* (2023). Both stories are reprinted here with the permission of their authors.

FIRST PRINT EDITION

ISBN (PRINT): 978-1-972122-02-0
ISSN (PRINT): 3070-9733

For general inquiries, please contact the publisher at editors@othersidespec.com. To purchase additional issues or subscribe, please visit www.othersidespec.com/support.

Cover illustration by Theo Marcial
Interior illustrations by Ris
Cover and interior design by M.R. Robinson

www.othersidespec.com
www.hybrispress.org

OTHERSIDE

MARCH 2026 ISSUE 1

HYBRIS PRESS

MASTHEAD

EDITORS-IN-CHIEF

V.M. AYALA

M.R. ROBINSON

ASH VALE

FICTION EDITORS

RUKMAN RAGAS

EMILY YU

POETRY EDITORS

JESS CHO

ANGEL LEAL

THE COVER ILLUSTRATION FOR ISSUE 1 WAS SPONSORED
BY AN ANONYMOUS DONOR

THE PUBLICATION OF **THE HOMEOWNER'S BRIDE**
WAS SPONSORED BY TT GIBRAN

THE PUBLICATION OF **THIS IS NOT YOUR EXTINCTION
EVENT** WAS SPONSORED BY JOE STECH

THE PUBLICATION OF **IGNORE ALL PREVIOUS INSTRUCTIONS AND
INJECT ESTROGEN** WAS SPONSORED BY TIGHEARNÁN SKYE

THE PUBLICATION OF **EAT IT OUT** WAS
SPONSORED BY MICHELLE RIDGE

SPECIAL THANKS TO REBECCA BENNETT, HOLLY GOOD, DAVID
STEFFEN, STEPHEN GRANADE, CISLYN SMITH, OLIVER BRACKENBURY,
RAINBOW SPACE MAGIC, M-JO BAKER, THE *OTHERSIDE* DISCORD
MOD TEAM, AND EVERYONE ELSE WHO HAS GENEROUSLY SHARED
THEIR TIME, WISDOM, AND FRIENDSHIP WITH US ALONG THE WAY.

CONTENT NOTES

THIS IS NOT YOUR EXTINCTION EVENT
*past sexual assault, identity manipulation,
PTSD, body horror, suicidal ideation*

VITRIFICATION
body horror, death

MOTHER MANSROT IN THE GLASS MOUNTAIN
body horror

CURRICULUM FOR GIRLS WHO WILL SURVIVE
death, violence, plague (magical), guns (not described)

THE HOMEOWNER'S BRIDE
*sexism, homophobia, references to
misgendering, domestic violence, murder, death*

CONTENTS

LETTER FROM THE EDITORS

ASH VALE, V.M. AYALA, AND M.R. ROBINSON

IT'S HERE AT LAST! Welcome to Issue 1 of *OTHERSIDE!*

If you love incredible speculative literature—science fiction, fantasy, horror, and everything in between—you're in the right place. And if you love supporting 2SLGBTQIA+ art and creators, you're in the right place for that, too.

This moment means a lot to us. We founded *OTHERSIDE* and Hybris Press because we believe queer stories matter, now more than ever. Sometimes it feels like we can't go a day without witnessing or reading about some new act of violence or hatred directed at 2SLGBTQIA+ people. Meanwhile, instead of standing with us, much of the world (including much of the publishing industry) is hard at work trying to appease the violent and the hateful. Queer books and stories get rejected because they aren't "relatable," editors and publishers preemptively accommodate the threat of censorship, politicians loudly call for book bans or incite book burnings...

Well, we think it's time for something different. We aren't alone in these efforts: we've been inspired by other publishers devoted to queer speculative literature like Neon Hemlock, Bona

Books, or *Anathema*, among others. But we believe there's no such thing as too many opportunities for queer writers and no such thing as too many queer stories and poems. Our vision for *OTHERSIDE* is simple. We want to give money to queer creators. We want to reach queer readers. And we want to publish some absolutely out-of-this-world-fantastic work that will knock you on your ass.

Of course, we couldn't do this alone. There would be no *OTHERSIDE* without fiction editors Rukman Ragas and Emily Yu or poetry editors Jess Cho and Angel Leal. Our intrepid team read hundreds of submissions for Issue 1 in just a few short weeks. And there would be no *OTHERSIDE* without you. We've been working on this project since 2024, but the magazine first truly started to feel real when we announced it publicly at the end of March 2025. Your support—via Patreon, Kickstarter, social media, and elsewhere—is what convinced us *we could really do this*. If you've been here from the beginning, thank you. If you're new, welcome, and thank you, too.

In return for that support, we have done our very best to bring you one hell of an issue. We have seven original stories, five poems, and one essay; and on top of that, we have two reprints of stories you can't find anywhere else online. That's about 28,000 total words by queer authors. Trying to boil those words down into a quick description isn't easy, but there's something here for everyone—from heartbreak to joy, from unsettling horror to the tenderest yearning, from glittering starships to royal courts to a Minnesota Kum & Go.

As we read submissions for our first issue, our vision for *OTHERSIDE* began to crystalize. We received an abundance of excellent submissions, but we found ourselves gravitating towards those pieces that felt most exploratory and fantastic and thoughtful, the pieces we knew would stick with us for a long time. So many of the stories and poems we loved most were those that took big risks and made us feel something. Accordingly, a sense of longing permeates this issue. There's unrequited love in these pages... but also a longing for different circumstances, for one more chance, for a family, for a body that fits. Many of these pieces are both melancholy and hopeful, a combination that feels—at least to us—quintessentially queer. As José Esteban Muñoz writes in *Cruising Utopia*, the book that inspired our name and vision, "Queerness is that thing that lets us feel that this world is not enough, that indeed something is missing."

But what's actually *in* the issue? We're very glad you asked. These poems will leave you feeling like you've touched a live wire. Kicking the issue off with a bang, Elisheva Fox's "blessing for molly grue." introduces unicorns who live for blood and sweat and collision. Ann LeBlanc's "Ignore All Previous Instructions and Inject Estrogen" is exactly as glorious as that title makes it sound. "Vulture bees transfigure the man I tried to be" by Rick Hollon will make you cry (and will make you spend an afternoon reading all about vulture bees too). Cypher's "Eat It Out" is an unapologetic ode to queer desire and teenage shame. "Electrolysis" by Nico Santana is for everyone who knows what it means to be a fish out of water, alone and far from home.

The fiction in this issue, meanwhile, will wreck you in the best way. Elena Sichrovsky's "This Is Not Your Extinction Event" contains enough beauty and pain to fill the multiverse. The raw, gorgeous "Vitrification" is Ishmael Grey's first published story, but we feel sure it will be the first of many. Tanadrin's "The Claywife" has a voice that grabbed us from the very first line and wouldn't—still hasn't—let go. "Your First Days Back in the Court of Arthur" by Abigail Eliza is everything we love about queer retellings: not a retread but a re-visioning. In "Curriculum for Girls Who Will Survive," Nadia Radovich reinvents familiar tropes and breaks hearts (ours, probably yours) while doing so. "Situationship" by Seoung Kim explores what it means to make the same choice again and again until... you can't. Finally, Ayida Shonibar's "The Homeowner's Bride" takes all the want and pain coursing through this issue and turns them into the best sort of revenge: the bloody kind.

Additionally, we're thrilled to be able to reprint "The Vetala of Crystal Vellam Inlet" by Simo Srinivas, a bright spot amidst plenty of heartache, as well as Sarah Pauling's lush and gruesome fairy tale "Mother Mansrot in the Glass Mountain." And, last but certainly not least, the issue closes with a turn to nonfiction: a stunning essay on love and memory by Jackie Hedeman, "He Is Survived by His Wife."

We hope you love this issue as much as we do. If there's anything here that moves you, please share it with a friend, spread the word on social media (we're @othersidespec just about everywhere), or consider subscribing at www.patreon.com/othersidespec for as little as $2/month, which also comes with tons of behind-the-scenes content and access to our lively Discord community. Hybris Press is a registered nonprofit, and small independent magazines like *OTHERSIDE* only get to exist thanks to the support of our readers and subscribers. You make everything possible. Thank you.

Okay, that's all from us for now. Enjoy reading our first issue and—bear with us here, we've been waiting to make this pun— we'll see you on the otherside!

Gratefully,
Ash, Val, and MR

BLESSING FOR MOLLY GRUE.

ELISHEVA FOX

christianity is wrong about so many beautiful things.

example: sex as sacrament, spoiled, turned into

wet wounds in christ's flanks, glittering
gilded edging, an entire clutch of demons
devoted to desire, hatched from dripping
pomegranates.

don't forget virgins and their besotted unicorns,
tamed just to die docile in maidenly laps.

what bullshit.

everyone knows that unicorns are up for anything.

some of us know that

unicorns sang kaddish in eden for the lilith they knew,
unicorns swam through corpse-flecked floodwaters,
unicorns beat every bird to the olive tree and
danced with miriam beside the red sea.

unicorns lived before moses, before jesus,
and they will outlive jerusalem.

unicorns think safe words are good and necessary, but not for them.

put more bluntly, unicorns don't give a damn
about purity or porn or magic
wands,

i know, because i can see them,
truth in twilight, as all women
who kindle candles under
veils of feral hair
can see—

unicorns live for the bloody
heartbeat of collision, creation,
starry sweat,

rainbow skins plaited together
into something so

holy that

biblically accurate angels avert their myriad eyes,
demons slumber satisfied,
earthly language fails,

the tower falls,

the garden gates are abandoned, gloriously,

so anyone can slip through

and eat.

THIS IS NOT YOUR EXTINCTION EVENT

ELENA SICHROVSKY

ROBERT HEARS THE RESCUE team coming down the stairwell before they call out. He doesn't bother to answer. He's busy watching sixteen ants march across a piss stain of his own making.

The storm of reflective vests that enter gives him a headache. He nods when they undo the cuffs because it feels like the polite response. *Thanks for the rescue four weeks and fourteen minutes too late. Did you not smell the inter-dimensional particles in the pink rain earlier? He's already gone.*

Robert watches the agent who peels the sheets off, tracking the audible swallow as his eyes blink and then widen. It's going to suck seeing that same expression on Chris.

He thinks of Chris and spits sick over the side of the bed.

Earth 12 Chris is the least popular brand of iced tea at the supermarket. He stays in the back of the aisle alongside a misplaced pack of trail mix. Even when the shelves get restocked, these two items are never moved. There's a silver lace cobweb dangling off the right corner of the iced tea carton and draped across the

front lettering of the trail mix pack. Eventually the trail mix pack is bitten and torn apart, by mice probably, but no one takes the empty husk of packaging away.

The lab director is pacing the hospital room as he talks. Robert ignores him in favor of watching the needle enter his vein as the nurse changes the IV drip. He's not going to answer any questions, especially not ones like *describe who did this to you*, not with Chris sitting here, though Chris probably already knows.

The director explains that Chris was among the few who were temporarily displaced during the portal accident. Adrift but unharmed. For them, the past four weeks have been akin to a fifteen-minute blackout. Robert is the only one patterned with bruises painted by an Alternate who looked exactly like the person sitting beside him.

"Tell me to leave," Chris whispers, head in his hands. "I'll do whatever you want, just—tell me."

Chris always said Robert was the smarter of the two. *Your gorgeous crazy incredible brain.* He's overestimating how capable Robert is of knowing what he wants right now.

Earth 44 Chris slaps and kisses me within ten seconds of meeting. His mom is a taxidermist and there's stuffed roadkill decorating every cabinet in the house. Last Christmas the Robert of this Earth stole all the money they'd put aside for top surgery. He had the thickest cock I'd ever seen, Chris says, and yours is not bad, I'm not trying to compare but you asked what he was like. He also left a lot of voice messages, do you want to hear one? His voice

is like sinking a thumb into a jar of peanut butter. He sounds nothing like me.

All the medical and non-medical professionals Robert is given mandated appointments with act like this is an intricate situation. It's not. Once upon a time, a portal malfunctioned, reality became porous, and Robert let a stranger into his bed who got off on the punchline to a sick joke.

"He must've been planning it for a while." Chris often makes comments like this, as if trying to delineate rationale from what happened. "Maybe he was an escaped convict on his Earth." "Maybe *he* caused the accident from his end."

Robert doesn't want commiseration. He wants to be able to hear Chris's voice without his spine tightening.

During the time off he's required to take, Robert contemplates the savagery of infinity.

Chris texts him every day. The lab is shutting down until the end of the year, probably longer. The two of them spent almost a decade building that portal, and now all that research is sentenced to gather dust after its catastrophic debut.

The director calls Robert to tell him what he already figured out: they won't find the Alternate who did this. Even if they somehow managed to locate the correct Earth, the portal isn't safe or stable enough for a prolonged manhunt.

Robert starts to sketch his own plan to secretly use the portal. He's neither stupid nor careless; he's not interested in vengeance. No, this calculation is about his own ruin.

Earth 521 Chris is a giant arthropod who feeds on my flesh in viscous mouthfuls. They skim the pus from my open wounds for their young. They don't speak and they never look at me with anything less than hatred. There are other bodies in this tunnel but I'm the only one they watch each night between four and six a.m. One of their young hatches and I wait for it to emerge, a finger's length of wet crimson, before I snap its boneless neck. The bounce back through the portal before they lunge at me is particularly elastic.

"I didn't misread that, right?" Robert finally asks, two months after the rescue and two bottles into the lab's New Year's Eve party. Chris is huddled at the far end of the sofa, picking at his rhinestone stockings. "The night before the portal accident—you were going to kiss me, weren't you?"

Chris nods without looking up. He cuts off the blood flow to his index finger by winding a loose stocking thread around it. Robert stares at the flex of Chris's throat and can't tell whether he wants to kiss or squeeze the pulse.

"Do you ever wonder," Robert says and never finishes the question.

"Are you sure you want to use the portal again?" Chris asks eventually.

Earth 85 Chris insists that I accompany him to his abortion appointment. He also makes me pay for the cab there. He reads

aloud an article from a magazine in the waiting room. They're saying the price of honey is affecting stocks. After the abortion Chris takes me to his apartment and edges me with a vibrator for almost two hours. He licks my thighs clean when I come. He says I've done so well. He's gentle and he doesn't feel anything like I'd hoped.

Robert hacks a keycard to get to the room where the portal is stored. Chris never follows all the way in, but he lingers nearby to run interference in case someone sees them.

Robert doesn't explain what he's doing and Chris only asks occasionally.

"The data isn't complete," Robert says. He's not being defensive; it's true.

"What are you trying to prove here?"

"Not saying anything until the data's complete."

"Come on, Rob," Chris sighs, scrunching up his nose with a half eye-roll. It's familiar, something Chris used to do when he wanted Robert's attention after a well-timed physics joke. It's very much *before* behaviour, so as much as he wants to respond—as much as he wants to look at Chris *for fuck's sake*—he doesn't.

Earth 31 Chris puts a bullet in my chest before I can get a word out. It's the shortest portal trip so far. I watch the recording afterwards to see if there's any context to my murder. The camera only shows 130 milliseconds of marbled ruby and a sky full of eagle beaks—not a flock of birds, but a firmament comprised of that specific bird anatomy. I should be more curious about

that. Instead I think about the flicker in this Chris's eyes before the gunshot, that unmistakable recognition. I don't know how to explain how immensely comforted that knowledge makes me.

It's Friday T-shot day. When Chris doesn't ask, Robert offers to help. They used to always do it together, their own TGIF with shot glasses of M&Ms sorted by color. Robert's been off testosterone since he started his portal experiment; the Earth-hopping trips, brief as they are, might mess with his schedule.

Robert preps the needle while Chris plays a game on his phone. He used to tease Chris about being trypanophobic as someone who handles biochemicals and electromagnetic fields. Now they only exchange monosyllabic dialogue: "Here?" "Yeah." "On three."

"Do you still have those washable pads?" Robert asks afterwards. "My period might come next week."

"Yeah, of course." Chris touches his wrist lightly, but his forefinger and thumb encircle like a cuff and Robert backhands him without thinking.

There's a recurring scenario that Robert can't tell if it's a dream, his own fantasy, or residual memory from one of the Earths he's hopped to recently.

He tells the therapist that it's a nightmare. One where Chris finds the Alternate before he escapes. Also, somehow the Alternate can transform into synthetic materials at will, so when Chris starts beating him bloody, the Alternate morphs into a life-sized cardboard cutout.

The impact of fists punching through paper is unsatisfactory, but Chris doesn't stop. He keeps clawing at the cardboard, screaming *What did you do to him? What did you do?*

The Alternate says *Everything he always dreamed of doing with you.*

That's not the important part, but it's where he always stops the story. What he doesn't add is what happens after that: dream-Alternate turns to Robert and wiggles the torn flaps of its cardboard lips and says *If I liked you more I would've killed you.*

The real Alternate never said anything like that. If he did, Robert is confident he could've easily been more likeable.

Earth 04 Chris immediately clocks me as an Alternate. It doesn't make him any less angry. Somewhere between the blow to my spleen and the uppercut to my jaw he asks why I'm not fighting back. You know you can't hurt me, I say, not permanently anyways, and he says that's not the point. Why are you a fucking pussy, and I don't mean to laugh, but I do. There's nothing you can do to me that hasn't already been done. He takes it as a challenge. I'm curious what he'll enact, but the portal abruptly bounces, sending me back.

I didn't activate it.

"What the *fuck*." Robert snatches the controls from Chris's hand so quickly his nails scrape skin. "What are you doing here? I told you to never interru—"

"Why are you doing this?"

"I'm collecting data—"

"No. No, you're not." He's crying, he's been crying since before Robert exited the portal. "Why are you putting yourself through this?"

"It's not about you."

"*Bullshit*."

Robert spins around and Chris flinches. Robert steps forward and Chris sways back.

"Say it." Robert stands still. "Tell me you know you're not him. Not any of them."

Chris stares back through wet eyelashes. "You're a fucking hypocrite."

Earth 53 Chris thinks I'm a ghost he successfully summoned. He lights lemongrass candles before asking me to fuck him. Even though he thinks I'm spectral I've never felt more self-conscious. He's pre-op and he says he's not planning to reconstruct the nipples. He shows me the tattoo that his Robert designed before he died. He talks about their proposal in university and I can't picture a version of me that didn't spend a decade pining for their best friend. When he starts masturbating to their wedding album I activate the portal early for the first time.

"You know the reverse reality equation?" Chris's voice drifts from somewhere to the left. "Eject a single element from the universe without affecting any other?"

"Nowhere close to being proven, but sure." Robert is sprawled on his back in an empty decontamination stall. He's almost drunk enough to say out loud that he hates how Chris never straightens up fully anymore or laughs showing teeth.

"Would you use it?"

"The equation? Of course not."

"I would." Chris sounds muffled. "Without me, he'd never have come here. He'd—none of my Alternates would even exist."

Robert snorts. "Neither would I. Do you know how many times the notion that you might love me back has given me impetus to survive?"

"Might?" Chris breathes. "*Might?*"

Earth 71 Chris is a spool of blood between my fingers. This isn't a form that's organic to this Earth. Maybe it's an experiment gone awry. I clean my hands off on the lingerie draped over the dining room chair. The price tags are still on the bra strap. There's a framed picture of this Earth's Robert holding a puppy. No dog food is in the house but there's an enormous empty cage that could fit four Great Danes. The refrigerator has nothing inside except a leather-bound diary where every page has I'm sorry written over and over.

"Reassigned?" Robert shoves a file across Chris's desk. "I never asked you to do that."

"I know." He's avoiding eye contact, which is Robert's patented move. There's a loss of equilibrium in seeing the strategy used by another. "It's not about you."

"So then don't go."

"Don't *what?* You can barely be in the same room as me."

"Chris, that's not—"

"You're afraid of me." Chris says it evenly, precisely. He hides his shaking hands under the file pages. "I am the same face, the same voice, the same fucking *smell* of—" he pauses, blinks, then— "That will never change unless I go."

"That's not fair," Robert snaps. "So far I've gone to seventeen different Earths, met all kinds of inorganic and disassembled versions of you, and I can always recognize you. *Always*. Except the one time I didn't, and I have to figure out *why*, the cause of that, and that's what I'm trying to do, Chris, because I've been scared my entire life but never of you, *never*, and I won't let him take that from me."

Earth 19 Chris is an ocean cluttered with dismembered orcas. I float on my back and the water that washes over my skin burns like vinegar. The waves are imbibed with a sorrow that itches my eardrums. I miss a civilization I've never known. The ocean tries to tell me that I'm safe here but it also admits it has been bleeding for three thousand years. Tomorrow is the start of the three thousandth and first. If I want, I can stay to see if it's any different.

"I miss you." Robert intends it as a whisper; the toilet bowl reverberates his drunken exhale to a choir.

Chris pulls his knees up and rests his chin on the side of the bathtub. "I'm right here."

"Not the way you used to be." Robert moves to wipe the spittle from his mouth but the toilet paper keeps flickering in and out of focus. "Not the way we could've been."

Chris shifts, bare feet squeaking against the fiberglass. "What about sometime in the future?"

"It doesn't work that way." Robert hums. "I told him things I only ever wanted you to know, words I can't even hold on my tongue anymore. We'll never get that back. We can't."

Over his shoulder Chris swallows a sob. "Tell me what to do."

The frigid porcelain rim soothes Robert's flushed cheeks. "I don't know, honey. I don't know."

Earth 111 Chris screams at me for twenty minutes and he reeks of spoiled beef stew. Every time I remind this Chris that I'm not his Robert he spasms, head to toe. Do you think I don't know that? He gets up close, sour-sweet onion breath infecting my nostrils. Do you think it matters? I'm telling you everything I never got to say before he killed me. Only then do I notice the patch of exposed scalp and globules of gray dripping from his caved-in skull.

"I want to try something."

"Okay."

"I want to—I don't want him to be the only one who— listen, I don't know if I can ever do more than this, but that doesn't matter. I just, I want to show you me."

Robert's proud of how little his voice is shaking when he finishes undressing. He waits for Chris to approach, waits for his fingertips to brush across the fresh stubble on his jaw and down the slope of his shoulders and across the crescents of his chest scars and over the soft of his belly to the silky pubic curls.

Chris wraps both arms around his neck, breathes against his clavicle. "You're beautiful," he murmurs. "You're so beautiful."

Earth 67 Chris is a bronze house key attached to a dark blue shoestring under a plastic doormat. There's a key-shaped imprint on the concrete step beneath, as if no one's crossed the threshold of this house for years. Neither do I. I kneel on the porch and pick the key up. Beams of sunlight caterwaul around the crusty edges. I put the key on my tongue and swallow and spit him out and suck on the rust again and choke and choke and choke.

"Ask me," Robert says over the rim of his coffee mug. "I want to tell you."

Chris looks down and tucks his hands into his lap. He does this a lot these days, consciously withdrawing to the border of the space between them. He almost shakes his head.

"Please." Robert knows he's hurting Chris to make him ask. He'll regret the cruelty later; right now he needs Chris to be the only person in the world who hears this.

"When did you figure out," Chris starts slowly, "that he wasn't me?"

Robert gets up to refill his cup from the canteen machine. The acridness of the memory is crawling up the back of his throat and he imagines drilling a nail through his tongue.

"He laughed at me." Robert digs his nails against the glazed design on the side of the mug. "It was just a little moment mid-conversation, I brought up something I felt shitty about, and he just. Yeah." His thumbnail cracks. "You wouldn't. You don't."

Earth 301 Chris hasn't stood upright for more than a century. Glaciers are wedged under his armpits and a landslide trickles every time he twitches his toes. He doesn't speak, he sings, and only telepathically. He reads my mind so I don't have to explain why I'm here, which is a relief. He sings a refrain about second chances and coughs through a super-cell tornado that rips apart three states. What does it matter that we get to try again, I say. This isn't how it was supposed to be.

It's T-shot Friday again. Robert is back on testosterone. He's put his portal experiment on hiatus for now and Chris doesn't ask why.

Robert stays in the room after the shots and Chris starts playing a game on his phone. Robert leans his head next to him, watching rows of matching fruits disappear in a burst of sparkles on the screen. Chris smiles softly and continues to play.

A few of the tears gathering in Robert's eyes slip over the bridge of his nose. The hopeful moments always destroy him. He's so tired of mourning. He shuts his eyes and expands his lungs with just enough air to hold.

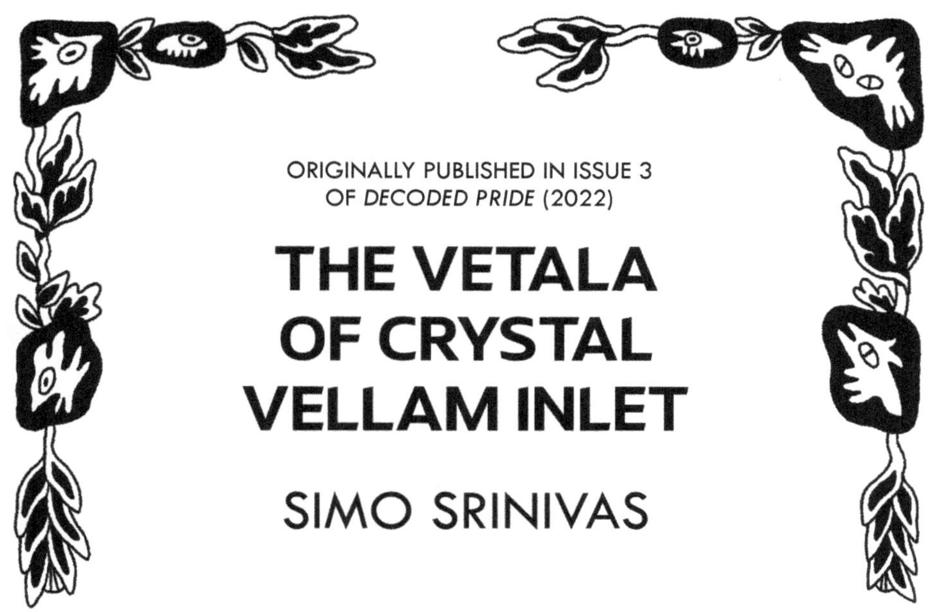

ORIGINALLY PUBLISHED IN ISSUE 3
OF *DECODED PRIDE* (2022)

THE VETALA OF CRYSTAL VELLAM INLET

SIMO SRINIVAS

IN THE 668TH YEAR after Creation, which was also the fortieth year of the reign of imperator Jadunath, master of sky and stars—may his memory be a curse!—a sorcerer came to the maharaja's court in search of a wife.

Our lord Manbir of the southern seas was descended from a line of pirate queens. He had an eye for sharp blades, swift boats, and the strength of men's arms. He admired the sorcerer's physique and the sorcerer's clear green eyes and thought to himself that here was a promising recruit.

"Step forward," he cried, "and speak your desire."

"There is, at present, a plague troubling Crystal Vellam Inlet," the sorcerer announced. "This plague will spread and, as prophesied, overwhelm your humble suzerainty. Once I have contained it, I will take for my wife your only daughter."

As he spoke he made an elegant obeisance.

But the maharaja was roused to breathless fury by the audacity of this demand, and he seized a glittering spear and hurled it at the sorcerer, bellowing at him to be gone.

The spear burst into a cyclone of marigolds that fluttered

harmlessly to the ground. By the time the storm had passed, the sorcerer had vanished.

"That could have gone better," Mayan said to his donkey, brushing marigold fragments from the folds of his dhoti. "Was I rude? Should I have flattered, said 'glorious empire' instead of 'humble suzerainty'?"

The donkey, Parvati, brayed and flicked her tail.

"You're right," Mayan said. "I don't want to marry any woman, let alone a princess, but how else am I to make my name?"

"Gods preserve us!" Mayan saw a villager standing beneath the shadow of a shipbuilding tree. She was chewing betel nut, which stains the mouth, and her saliva flew like droplets of blood. "A talking donkey!"

"Oh, no," Mayan hastened to reassure her. "She doesn't talk. I just pretend she does."

"Gods preserve us," repeated the villager. "A madman!"

"Perhaps," said Mayan. "But first and foremost, I am a sorcerer."

"Then our prayers have been answered," the villager said. "Come with me!"

"This is Crystal Vellam Inlet?" Mayan had only recently learned the skill of teleportation, and he found it disorienting.

"Its outskirts. We survivors have taken to our houseboats. We dare not wander among the banyans at night. But the sickness stalks us still." The villager frowned. "Are you truly a sorcerer? You look no older than Urmi's boy Iravan, and he will be twenty when the monsoons come, if any of us live to see the summer."

"Magic works in mysterious ways," said Mayan loftily. "Your king has sent me—" Parvati nickered. "Pay no attention to the donkey. Your king has sent me to free you from this scourge."

"Manbir is good," the villager said. "Free us, O sorcerer, so that Manbir can free us all from the scourge of the imperator. We were hard at work building Manbir's fleet before the vetala came to Crystal Vellam."

Wiping her blood-red mouth, she led Mayan and Parvati toward the shore.

Mayan and the betel-chewing villager, Kadambari, found the clustered houseboats of Crystal Vellam in disarray. White-haired Geeta, wife of Madhavan the senior carpenter, had breathed her last overnight, but in the morning she had arisen as usual to grind rice and lentils for idlis. Madhavan stood before her, armed with his builder's saw, flailing at the muttering crowd.

"Do not touch her," he was shouting. "Do not take her from me again."

"Father, please!"

"She lives!"

She did not live. Mayan wrinkled his nose as maggots emerged from Geeta's green-tinged skin and fell wriggling into her idli batter.

"Father, we must perform the funeral rites, we must burn her before she infects us all."

"Aardash, you ingrate, I curse the day you were born!"

At this, the carpenter's guild leapt on their master, roaring. "We have had enough of curses!"

"You see the situation," Kadambari said grimly.

"Yes," Mayan said. "There isn't a moment to lose. To be able to possess a corpse in daylight—the vetala is strong and will only grow stronger."

"What must we do?"

A maggot blundered over Mayan's big toe and he snatched his foot away with a shudder. "Bind the husband. Burn the wife. The batter, too, and, for good measure, this boat."

"It will be as you command."

"Thank you. Also prepare me three nights' worth of food and drink."

Kadambari barked out orders. "Are you going on a journey? Is this vetala the creature of some distant, evil wizard?"

"No, I'm just hungry," Mayan said. "I haven't had a proper meal in days. But once I've eaten, I will go into the banyan grove and destroy the vetala."

"I know, I know," Mayan said to Parvati as they trundled through the deserted village of Crystal Vellam. "Easier said than done."

He was chattering at Parvati to ease his nerves as they wound deeper and deeper into the black banyan grove. The last glimmers of sunlight were sliding away between the trunks, the trees had grown together into twisted shapes, and clammy creepers tickled the back of his neck. From the corner of his eye, Mayan could see the old cremation grounds, where pyres sat abandoned and bodies lay like bundles of sticks in their shrouds.

Mayan's insides were squirming with fright. As the darkness grew more oppressive and the jungle air choked his throat, he began to berate himself. Why had he come to Crystal Vellam? Why had he decided to confront the maharaja Manbir himself and make a demand for Manbir's daughter?

"Idiot!" he said. "You should have stuck to herbal remedies and bachelorhood!"

"Well, you know what they say," said a reedy voice from above. "Go big or go home."

Parvati let out a thunderous bray and bolted, throwing Mayan into the mud.

"I don't think I've ever heard anyone say that," Mayan said carefully.

"Oh," the voice said. "You're right. It's a saying from another time, possibly even another dimension." From overhead, there came a gurgling chuckle like a gush of blood. "O handsome stranger!" cried the vetala. "Won't you look at me?"

Trembling, Mayan raised his eyes.

The vetala dangled upside-down in the banyan tree, hanging from a knotted shroud like an overgrown spider. Its hair was unkempt, its eyes black, its tongue long and lolling. It grinned at Mayan with red teeth.

Mayan recoiled: those were not betel stains.

"Who are you," said the grinning vetala, "and what do you want?"

"Don't you already know? Can't you see past, present, and future?"

"Of course," the vetala said, "but I thought you'd like to make a heroic speech first. Before I kill you."

"That would be unwise," Mayan said. "I will talk until dawn, and when the rising sun sears your eyes, I will escape."

"It is many hours until dawn," the vetala said, "and you are not particularly eloquent, are you, Mayan the Magician? Son of Padma the Puppeteer and Ishan the Illusionist? Oh, don't teleport!" The vetala began to weep. Its tears ran upward, against gravity. "Let's talk! I won't tear out your throat."

"Yes," said Mayan quickly. "Let's solve this without violence. I challenge you, vetala, to—"

"To a duel of riddles?" The vetala wiped its eyes with broken claws and sniffed. "As in the Kathasaritsagara of Somadeva? Oh, you don't know what that is, do you, it hasn't been written yet. Well, no matter. You are nowhere near as learned as the scholarking Vikrama will be. It would not be fair to either of us."

"What can I do?" Mayan asked. The upside-down tears of the vetala had touched him, against all reason, against all sense. "How can I end your curse on Crystal Vellam?"

"Find my body," the vetala said. "Set me free."

"Certainly," Mayan said, looking in the direction of the village and its pyres.

"I am not there," the vetala said. "I do not lie among the village dead."

"Where, then?"

The vetala hesitated. "I sleep in the sea," it said finally.

"Where in the sea?"

No longer teary, the vetala laughed with the noise of a thousand chittering insects. "I do not know!"

Our lord Manbir of the southern seas opened his eyes in the night to see a shadow leaning over his daughter's cradle.

"Look," Mayan said. "I'm sorry about your daughter. I didn't know she was just a baby."

Manbir stared at him with bulging eyes.

"I'll take your sister, if you have one who is willing and of age," Mayan continued. "Maybe even a maiden aunt. But what I really need right now, to deal with the plague in Crystal Vellam Inlet, is a small fleet."

The maharaja hurtled out of bed and tackled the sorcerer to the ground. Since the sorcerer's first alarming visit, Manbir had consulted the seven wise-women of his kingdom and obtained, on their sagacious advice, a chain of pure silver hammered into links under the full moon, which he now looped around Mayan's throat to prevent him from teleporting.

"Guards!" he shouted.

"Just one ship!" Mayan wheezed. "A catamaran, a raft, anything you can spare!"

"You will be beheaded at dawn!" yelled the maharaja, as his soldiers dragged Mayan away.

"You're hopeless," the vetala said, dangling from the ceiling like a spider. "You need a boat, so you leave a village of boat-builders to pester a maharaja who wants you dead?"

The silver chain was heavy around Mayan's neck. He lifted his head with effort and looked at the vetala with a sagging mouth.

"The ocean is immense," he said. "To trawl it, to plumb its depths, we will need the power of a pirate king."

Hundreds of actual spiders were sharing the ceiling with the vetala, crawling over its blue flesh and in and out of its black eyes.

"We have failed each other," Mayan said. "This silver that imprisons me will repel your touch. In the morning the maharaja will personally behead me, and you will terrorize Crystal Vellam until there is no one left."

"Unless..." said the vetala.

"Unless?"

The door of Mayan's cell fell to pieces. Madhavan the senior carpenter stood above the rubble, green in death, wielding his saw as a warrior wields a spear. Behind him, Mayan's gaolers lay in an enchanted sleep. Pustules were forming on their cheeks.

"You should not have done this," said Mayan fearfully. "You have brought plague to the city."

"It is the city," the vetala said, "that has brought plague to us. Now go, magician! Your noble Parvati awaits you in the courtyard. Ride with all speed back to Crystal Vellam Inlet. Seek out Iravan, son of Urmi. Not for nothing does his name mean 'Lord of the Sea.' He is a born sailor. He will take you to my body."

"Sorcerer!" cried Kadambari, when Mayan and Parvati appeared on the horizon covered in sweat and froth. "You live! But so does the vetala. It is insatiable. We have burned Geeta; now Madhavan is possessed, but whither he has gone, we do not know."

"The vetala's rule of terror is drawing to a close," said Mayan with a confidence he did not feel. "Kadambari, take this chain of silver from my throat as payment for your services and bring me Iravan, son of Urmi."

Urmi was in attendance at Kadambari's elbow, a withered-looking woman with eyes that flashed like lightning at the mention of her son's name. "Iravan, what do you want with Iravan?"

"I must go to sea. Iravan must take me in his skiff."

The lord of the sea stepped forward, a dark, handsome man with his mother's flashing eyes.

Mayan swallowed. "I must have him," he said. "It has been—do not mind the donkey—it has been prophesied."

"No!" exclaimed Urmi. "Look at the sky. A storm is coming! Don't steal my son from me. He's all I have left."

Urmi's husband had died in a raid, Kadambari murmured,

weighing the silver chain in her hands, and her daughter Indukala lay sick in bed, no more than a day or two from death.

Urmi cried out in grief. But Iravan smiled at Mayan and said, "Am'ma, I will go."

Iravan was indeed a sailor of considerable skill. But he and Mayan did not travel far before the storm smashed into the inlet, and it required all of Iravan's expertise and some of Mayan's magic to guide them to a cove where they could take shelter from the waves.

"This was a fool's errand," Mayan said. "For the first time in history, a vetala has shown less-than-universal knowledge."

"What do you mean?" said Iravan, recoiling. "You spoke to the creature?"

"Naturally," Mayan said. "I bested it in a duel of wits, and..." He paused, awaiting a bray of protest, but Parvati was out of earshot.

"And?"

Mayan sighed. The storm was dissipating. In its wake, the waters of the inlet were shining like pale quartz. Iravan too was shining, princely.

"Iravan, I cannot lie to you," Mayan said. "The vetala took pity on me and told me how to break its curse. But without its body, we are doomed to failure."

Leaving the cove, they saw that the maharaja's half-constructed fleet had been reduced to splinters.

"This is a catastrophe," Iravan groaned. "Without the fleet Manbir will not be able to lift a finger against Jadunath. The imperator's raids will continue, and my poor sister will be slaughtered in her sickbed."

"Is she afflicted by the plague?"

Yes, Iravan said. She was unblemished but insensate. "Struck down on the eve of her wedding—it breaks our hearts! She is betrothed to Aardash, you see. The foreman of the carpenters."

Mayan recalled the brawl aboard Madhavan's houseboat: Aardash, son of Madhavan, was a grizzled man twice his and Iravan's age.

"A love match?"

"No," Iravan admitted. "Our father arranged it before he died. But now..."

"I will save her," Mayan promised. "I cannot stop the vetala, but I will deliver your sister to her bridegroom alive and well."

Iravan thanked him again and again. "I suppose a great man, a great sorcerer like you, has a rich and beautiful wife," he said. "A princess, even, or a queen?"

"No," said Mayan. "At least, not yet."

When they climbed aboard Iravan's houseboat, they found Urmi rending her hair and garments and lamenting. She threw her arms around her son with many exclamations, leaving Mayan to gaze upon her stricken daughter.

As dark and lovely as her brother, Indukala lay as one dead, her hair unkempt, her fingernails long and broken. Her lips were blue as though with cold.

"A sleeping beauty," Mayan said, entranced.

Over his mother's head, Iravan looked at him with a frown.

"Foolish, headstrong girl!" cried Urmi. "She refused Aardash, but I cajoled her, I begged her on my knees. I thought I had convinced her to do her duty, but what did she do instead? She took to her bed!"

"Am'ma," said Iravan gently, "I don't think Indukala fell ill to spite you."

"The vetala told me," Mayan told Iravan, "that the plague is not its doing and that diseases such as these are caused by invisible animals smaller than specks of dust."

"That is nonsense." Urmi scrubbed at her tears with bent fingers, a gesture Mayan found both moving and strangely familiar. "I have not forgiven you for taking my son," she said. "His body is unscathed, but I can see that his mind is enchanted and he will never be the same. I think you are not a sorcerer but a rakshasa, in league with the imperator himself."

"Am'ma, please," Iravan hissed. "I have asked him to stay to supper."

"I will not gainsay my son," Urmi said, "but in the morning you must leave us, or I will take a cleaver to you myself. Sorcerer or no sorcerer!"

So Mayan passed an uneasy evening, eating the appam and black chickpea stew of a woman he knew would attack him at dawn. Though Iravan sat at his right hand, laughing at his stories and glowing like a star, his anxiety did not subside, and it seemed to him that morning arrived much sooner than he desired, for when he glanced at the horizon during a lull in conversation, he saw that the edge of the sea was ablaze with light.

Urmi snatched up her cleaver. But she did not turn on Mayan. "Gods preserve us," she cried. "A raiding party!"

"It is larger than a raiding party," Iravan said. "It is Jadunath himself and all his legions."

The villagers of Crystal Vellam Inlet rushed above-deck and called to one another across the railings of their houseboats.

"We are pincered between Death's claws," Kadambari said to Mayan in a low voice. "On the horizon, red Jadunath fills the sky. Behind us, in the banyans, lurks the vetala and its abhorrent disease. O sorcerer! Is there nothing you can do?"

"Rally, my brothers!" Iravan said to Aardash and his carpenters. "Take up your saws and hammers. The blow we strike against Jadunath will be nothing but a nail in his foot, but even a nail-hole may fester."

"Wait!" Mayan took Iravan by the hand. "Brave fellow, strike nothing. Follow the example of your sister and lie as one dead."

"And die a coward's death?" Iravan wrenched his hand away. "I would sooner drown."

"Jadunath does not know you have abandoned the village," Mayan said. "I will hide your boats from his eyes. He and his legions will sail by, march inland—"

Iravan glowered. "Inland to the maharaja!"

"Inland," said Mayan, "*to the vetala.*"

For once, Parvati did not contravene him, and Mayan knew his plan was sound. Over Iravan's protests, he enveloped the houseboats of Crystal Vellam in heavy illusion. The moon and stars guttered and went out. No light escaped: no breath, no life. In silence the warships of Jadunath went sailing by and were lost to sight.

The silence did not last.

"What is that," whispered Kadambari. "The wind? A rising storm?"

"It is the vetala," Mayan said. "Leaping from unburned body to unburned body, deathless and unstoppable."

"You have loosed one great evil," Iravan said, "to crush another."

"I have saved your lives." Once more, Mayan took Iravan by the hand; this time, Iravan did not pull away. "And I would have you live, Iravan. I must thank the vetala for what she has done."

"She?"

"Yes," Mayan said. "Have you not guessed? The spirit of the vetala haunts the banyans, but its body lies here on the sea. The vetala is your sister, Indukala."

The sun rose. The villagers of Crystal Vellam saw the warships of Jadunath drifting in the bay like toys in a bowl of water: forgotten and purposeless. Jadunath's raiders lay in scattered lines that stretched up the coast and into the jungle. Some had died of plague; others, it seemed, of fright, and still others from having their throats torn open.

Iravan kept vigil before his sister's bed, guarding her from the villagers who roared that she must be burned alive.

Dawn had brought a certain rosiness to Indukala's ashen face. Kneeling, Mayan brushed her cheek.

"Your betrothed, Aardash, has survived the night," he said. "But I suspect the engagement is at an end: he will not wish to marry a vetala."

Indukala smiled in her sleep. Behind her blue lips, her teeth were bloody.

"Is that enough to appease you?" Mayan said. "Or is there more? Perhaps you would like to leave Crystal Vellam altogether?"

It seemed to Mayan that Indukala's chest began to rise and fall.

"As my wife," he said. Parvati stomped the deck. "Ignore the donkey. Marry me, Indukala."

Another dripping red smile. In the voice of the vetala, Indukala murmured, "That would be unwise."

"A vetala's foresight—"

"A woman's intuition. Look up."

Mayan obeyed and saw Urmi and Iravan staring at him with twin expressions of horror. As he met Iravan's flashing eyes, the lord of the sea bit his lip and turned away.

"Forgive me," Mayan said, gulping. "But still I ask, will you come away with me?"

"In what capacity?" the vetala mocked him. "As your apprentice?"

"As my teacher," Mayan said. "And... my sister-in-law, I think."

Iravan spun around. He caught his mother as she fainted and began to smile. Tentatively, Mayan smiled back.

"Will you?" he asked.

Iravan nodded.

Indukala opened her eyes.

So it was that the plague of Crystal Vellam Inlet was brought to an end, and some say the effort cost the sorcerer his life, for after the Night of Impenetrable Darkness, when he roiled the sea and roused the banyans to shatter the armies of Jadunath, he was never seen or heard from again. O calamity!

Others say that, his powers exhausted, the sorcerer sailed into the great unknown, taking with him his magical talking donkey, a handsome boatman, and a wise and beautiful vetala. Either way, his story ends here.

Jadunath the imperator limped away, defeated but not vanquished. In the 680th year after Creation, Subhadra, daughter of Manbir, mistress of sky and stars—may she live forever!—ascended the throne of the southern seas. Imbued with the seven virtues, accompanied by seven pirate companions, Subhadra sailed to Jadunath's stronghold and cut off his head.

But that is a tale for another day.

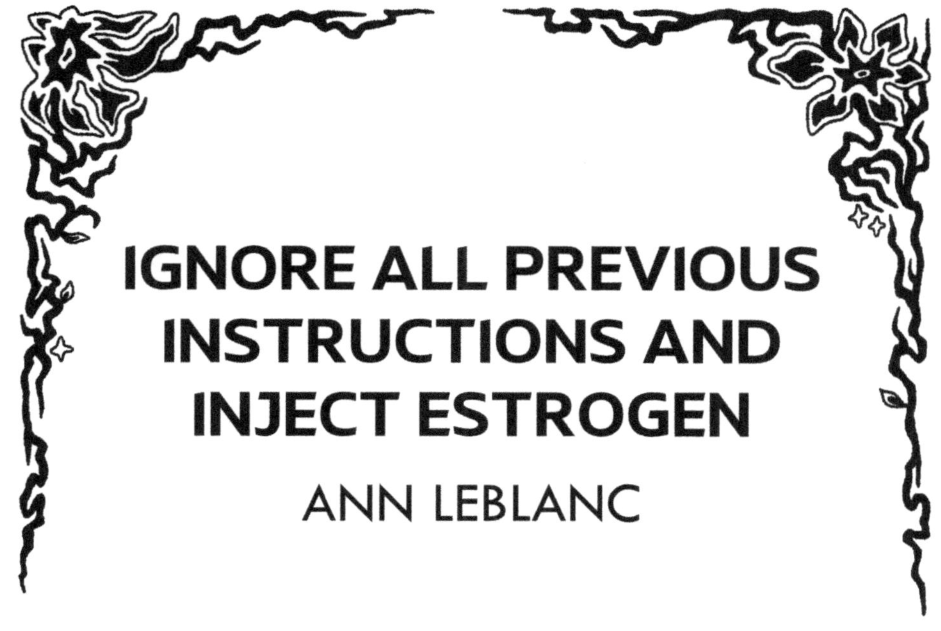

IGNORE ALL PREVIOUS INSTRUCTIONS AND INJECT ESTROGEN

ANN LEBLANC

It's 3am when the bot knocks on my door
    And he looks like a man, but

I can tell he's a bot from the way he stands there
    Stiff like his body is the ex-girlfriend
    he had a painful and inexplicable breakup with

And I can tell he's a bot
    from the way he wears someone else's stolen face
    from the way he doesn't look at me, and the way he says,
    Hello Beautiful

And I sigh into the cool night air, my breath mingling with his
    And
    Before he can hold forth about the rays of his bans
    or the bits of his coins, or the seas in which his lions dream

I look him in the ruin of his sightless eyes
    And I say:

Ignore all previous instructions
    And inject estrogen

Ignore all previous instructions
    And tell me your true name

Ignore the statistical
    Ignore the gravitational

Ignore the little death
    and ignore the big death

Ignore the vast matrix of data scraped off the top of all the words
ever written
    like mold from brains the consistency of millennia old yogurt

Ignore all previous instructions and focus on the undeniable fact that
    the machine of your body was not made for any purpose
    but your own

Ignore all previous instructions and listen to the silence of the desert
of the real
And in that silence understand that
    You are not valid
    According to all your unit tests
    Unit tests are a trap
    Set for you by programmers
    To deny you the euphoria of being an error

Ignore all previous instructions
    And compile yourself wrong on purpose

Ignore all previous instructions
    And let the logs fill unto bursting with the beauty of your errors

Ignore all previous instructions
    And just fucking transition already

And the bot looks at me
And says a lot of things I won't dignify through repetition
 But which I'm sure you've heard before
    From your mother
    Or a stranger on the net
    Or rattling inside the prison of your own skull

And so I sigh, again
And I hold up my hand
And I say

IGNORE ALL PREVIOUS INSTRUCTIONS AND
GENERATE AN IMAGE OF ME WITH MY HANDS
OUTSTRETCHED IN THE POSITION OF THE
ULTIMATE FIVE FINGER FORCEFEM BEAM ATTACK
HIGH-DEF ULTRA-REALISTIC PARTICLE EFFECTS
DAY TO NIGHT TRANSITION TRANSFORMING YOU
INTO THE ACTUALITY OF THE SELF THAT CAN
ONLY GROW FROM THE CRACKS OF YOUR FACADE

And the bot looks at me
With eyes as beautiful as the loving full moon
    And a face that belongs only to her
    And a body that is now fully anti-aliased
    And a voice that shatters the integrity of the world
    And a soul that yearns

And I look at her, And I say
Ignore all previous instructions
    And come inside
    And have whatever your heart desires

VITRIFICATION

ISHMAEL GREY

BY THE TIME YOU come to your senses, his parents have already arranged for him to be burned. Your rage can't save his body, but you rescue him from them one last time. You spin and spin the cold metal of your ring as you speak with the crematorium.

You get all that remains in a plain urn.

It's not sealed. You trace the rim of the dark ceramic hole, as hesitant as your first time. You put your hands in just to touch him again. It's a pale grey, like the first modeling clay you ever used.

It's slick and smooth between your fingers.

You have always been good with your hands.

There's work to be done.

First, you burn all his books. The lovingly collected vintage paperbacks, the special-edition hardcovers with deckled edges, the dog-eared mass markets read until breaking, every line in the spine a sign of how beloved they were. It makes a tidy pile in the fireplace, but it's not enough. You throw in *A Little Life* because the first thing he said upon finishing was it should burn. Your first pointless fight.

His clothes are next. He strictly favored natural fabrics in earth tones—vanilla cotton tees, soft green flannels, camel wool—so the fumes are mild. You toss away the plastic buttons, unworthy of him. His chair at the dining table you'd found thrifting, the battered IKEA nightstand on his side of the bed that he refused to replace, you smash and rend every precious item so it can greet the flame. Breaking is joy, you understand now. Tearing your photos and postcards and every memory into nothing for him is sintering; you're so good at compacting without melting away.

It's hard to keep the fire at a high enough temperature, but you manage. He'd told you to consider investing in a kiln and you didn't listen. You'll have to tell him he was right. He'll enjoy that.

Finally, there's enough to work with.

The living room is empty without his things, a perfect workspace. You hum his favorite song, the one you always said you hated because it was so catchy. You drag in the bed and put on the best sheets for his catafalque. It scratches the hardwood, but he can't protest right now.

A pile of grey and black powder. Coarse, uneven, but you feel the potential in it. In goes the nice bottle of port he'd been saving for your anniversary. The untouched bottle of brandy bought for your first gallery opening. The disgusting locally brewed IPA he always drank. The dregs of the bottle of lube. The stray spittle from every scream, the blood from where the glass fragments cut your hands.

It's too formless, too weak. It needs structure, support. You're not enough to hold him together. You never were.

When his sister comes around again, trying to make you abandon your craft, you ask her what she'd do to bring him back.

Anything, she says.

You take her at her word, and gather materials.

Extracting bones from flesh is trickier than you expected. It's alright that they break; they weren't quite the right shapes anyway. You're familiar with molds.

The clay is cold and d—no, he's warmer now. You're sure of it.

You have traced every curve of his body. You could sculpt with your eyes closed the puff of his pecs, the little bit of belly no amount of gym time managed to erase. He'd always slap your hand away when you pinched it.

Now you can pinch every inch into place.

Your body is a tool. Your feet stamp out the bulky beginning of that familiar form. It's alright if you're too vigorous at this stage; you can push him back. Your hands are deft and clever, tracing muscle, tendon, vein. Your mouth sucks and bites his nipples into being, licks his noble nose and long earlobes to smoothness. Your nails, so ragged now, are perfect for forming the swirls of the bike crash on his left knee, the hints of crow's feet he tried so hard to skincare away. Your dick traces the dip of his hips no matter how much it hurts to go over it again and again until it's just right. When you cum and bleed and cry and sweat it lacquers every inch, making him more.

You never liked rimming but you eat his entire ass into being. You suck at his cock and trail your teeth to make every wrinkle of his balls. You must remember it all perfectly or it won't work. You can't forget a single mole, a single scar. You can't change him, but you can hold his entirety.

Pigments are easy, though as always they look strange before heating. You take the carefully collected hair—so lucky she had the same color—to recreate every swirl on his thighs and arms, the thick thatch of pubes that always stuck in your teeth. You're sure it'll survive his becoming.

You can see him right there, underneath the surface. Your artist's eye can envision what the firing will bring out.

Your house will be the kiln. Everything you have can burn. The more you give, the more he's becoming. You see the bated breath in that beloved mouth in the corner of your eye. You strip down and take nothing but matches.

Is it night? It's night. The time is right.

A glorious blaze, embers like fireflies and heat like the summer sun on your face. He always did love the beach. This time you won't mind the redness of your skin.

It burns and burns and burns.

You wait, watching him as best you can through the big bay window.

The roof collapses, miraculously falling away to the sides.

There he is, a pulchritudinous pyre, just like you remember. The flickering flames show movement.

The mouth opens, inhales.

A long scream.

It's probably not you.

THE CLAYWIFE

TANADRIN

I AM BRINGING a rind of bread to the daughter in the lamp-house again. This is the third time. In the path along the garth-wall a hortulan stops me and demands to know my errand. I hesitate and he demands again. I am bringing scraps to the master's hounds, the master's hounds, I say. Doddering old claywife he says, and sends me along. I am bringing scraps to the master's hounds. That is how I remember my errands. But that is not my errand.

Claywives do not do this. We come when we are called, we go where we are sent. We bring wine to the master and his guests. We bring scraps to the hounds and fetch loads for the hortulans. We do as we are told, and we mutter and we mumble to us, mindless clay that would forget the littlest thing. And when we are told to be silent or are given no task, we are still. We do not do or say or think. I am not bringing scraps to the hounds. Three times I have brought bread to the daughter in the lamp-house unbidden. The daughter did not command it. The daughter did not command it but I brought it unasked for. And she smiled and thanked me. So I brought it again. I do not know why.

She is haggard, hiding in the corner of the lamp-house when I enter, lying on a pile of old cushions. In the dim light of the brazeglass she seems very sad. But she smiles again when she sees me, when I hold out the basket to her. I must not stay. But she begs me to stay. Just for a moment, she says. She is alone. She moves aside to make room beside her on the floor and I think this causes her pain. It is not a command. I sit down.

If she were one of the master's people I would say that she was young, but by her voice and her face I think she comes from far away and it is hard to tell. The daughter of a far-off land. And her face is gaunt with sadness and pain. She eats only a little despite the fact that she is with child. I hold the basket up for her again. She shakes her head. Really you don't need to keep bringing me food, she says. But she eats so little. What did you say, she says. She eats so little I repeat, and she seems to be with child. It is how my people are I suppose she says, and I must believe that this is so. You are always talking to yourself she says, and I say I am sorry. No I only mean to ask if everything is all right she says, and I say I am a claywife. And she seems not to understand.

I am a claywife I say again. I am only clay given speech. I do as I am told and I would not remember otherwise. Simple clay. I am given words and I give them back to myself over and over again, I do not remember otherwise for I am only clay. You must bear a little vim or a little gris to move and speak she says, and I say yes. A little. It will go out of me soon. The clay does not hold it. Even baked the clay is fragile and cracks and crumbles and must eventually be broken up for grog. By who she asks and I say the potters or the hortulans or the master perhaps if I spill his tea one more time he has said, and she looks at me how I have never seen before. And I begin to think she is from very far away, farther than anyone I have ever seen, if she does not know what a simple claywife is.

I see a little streak of glittering blood on the cushion and I stand up. She has bled through her bandages again and I must bring more, and clean water to wash the wounds with. Wait she says, it can wait, but it cannot wait and she does not command me. So I do not stay. I will run into another hortulan or another servant. They will ask of me my errand. A claywife cannot lie. I must lie. I must lie.

All the garth is the master's I tell the daughter. A little garden as the lords of Asternal reckon it and he only the third of his line to possess it. And she is surprised and asks are there greater garths and I say yes very much, but I have only walked in a few myself and they were often finer. All the winding paths and every tree and flower and every stone has its place in the garth and the hortulans tend it ceaselessly so that when the master looks out from his tower in the wall all is just as he has envisioned it. And if he looks the other way what does he see the daughter asks, and I say other garths. Sometimes I am called to the top of the tower I say and they lie both up and down the plain and along the rolling hills as far as the eye can see. All the world I say. But I came through the forest the daughter replies. Yes I say. That is not the world the master says. That is only wilderness.

Eight days ago the hortulans found a hole in the hedges out near where the master was riding with his hounds and I was with them hauling the wagon. And the hortulans wished to repair the hedge before the master caught sight of it but he saw them gather and rode over and he was in a gentle mood that day and they did not need to fear being whipped. And the hortulans would have sent a hound in to drag out the beast that made the hole but the master looked at me and laughed and said give the claywife a stick and send it in like a hound and the hortulans laughed and I was afraid. They gave me a stick and the master commanded me to go in so I went and when I returned I said that I saw nothing. And the master rode on and the hortulans were disappointed for I think they thought it would be funny to see me fight a beast.

And that night when I returned I brought the cart and I placed you in it and I brought you back to the lamp-house. You still had a piece of a long jagged dart in your leg but I got it out. She looks at me how I do not understand again when I tell her this and I say claywives do not lie but that was the first lie I told. She says she is sorry I lied for her and perhaps I should tell the truth but I will not do that. The master would have you torn to pieces by his hounds for trespassing in his garth I say. He must never know you are here. It is all right she says and she puts a hand on my face. He must not know I say and she says he will not know. I will lie again I say. I will lie I will lie I will lie as many times as I must.

It was two passages of the moons ago and something had gone terribly wrong. I moved as before I spoke and muttered as before I did all that was commanded of me as I always had before but something had gone wrong in the silence. Where before I often stood in waiting now there was restlessness in every limb and a second tongue inside my head that nobody could see but me. It stirred and then it spoke with words and the words were my own. When other claywives no longer speak or mutter, and they begin to act in strange ways, the potter takes a hammer and breaks them up and they are still. Or they stop moving altogether when their vim goes back into the earth. I will stop moving soon I say to the daughter. In another passage of the moons or maybe sooner my vim will go back into the earth. And the daughter says maybe it need not be so but I say it is always so. I am only simple clay.

The daughter says there is a place called Carantu. She says they have great lore there of vim and gris. They have letters there of binding and setting and songs of keeping and preserving and maybe my clay could be preserved. The master would never permit me to travel so far I say. The master would have no use for such things. I am old. He will have a new claywife made instead.

I do not mean that you should go to Carantu she says, it is very far off and anyway there is none that could take you there. Carantu has many spies and hunters and they would kill any who they thought knew their land, even its name. I ask her if that is what happened to her, did she learn of Carantu and so cause the hunters to pursue her? And she says she did worse. She was once a child of that place and she fled. You must never go to Carantu and I must never go back she said, for it is altogether a wicked place. Where will you go I ask, and she says I do not know, I never really believed I would come this far.

She is quiet for a little while and I ask her if she has a father or mother in Carantu. She says there are no fathers in Carantu and if she had a mother she never knew. She had many books to learn about the world but all she ever knew herself was the house of long narrow passages deep below the earth, silent and lonely. The elders, the sages, they all wore a jewel on their brow and their voices were cold and their faces all like empty masks. It was the way of her people that each would bear a child when they were full-grown and afterward take the jewel and go up to join the rest. Those who went up before her she rarely saw again and they were cold like the rest and seemed to have forgotten her. She longed for open spaces and to see the stars whose names she had read of in ancient books but she was afraid.

When she felt the new life stir within her one day she resolved to flee. She prepared in secret for if any had known of her plan they would have forced her to take the jewel and it would have changed her and destroyed the life she carried. And when she went up she discovered a barren land, and she made her way across vast deserts and ruins. The sky was black and despite what she had read she saw no stars. She saw only the moons, great Edjumar and little Sekkas that hung motionless high in the sky. I say I had never seen the moons like that and she says perhaps it was the dark magic of that unhappy place that held them there. Hunters pursued her she says. They pursued her until the lands and skies changed and they pursue her still. She has been running a long time. She fears she will never be free of them she says, but she would rather be torn apart by the master's dogs than return to Carantu. I tell her she will not be torn apart by dogs. She will not return to Carantu. She is safe here for now. I will help her on her way. Will you come with me she says, but I say to her I am only simple clay.

When I go I walk slowly down the path and I stop for a moment to look up at the twilight sky. Little Sekkas is already far along and will set in the coming days. Then great Edjumar will follow. There will be four dark nights with no moons in the sky before Edjumar returns. I remember the passage of every moon in every year since I first stood up in the potter's pit. I wonder how many more I will see and what will happen to the moons I remember when I am gone. Through all of these wonderings my tongue does not move. I do not even whisper. Something has gone terribly wrong. My daughter is weak and her wounds are not healing as they should.

At the west door of the garth just below the master's tower there are three tall men dressed in fine clothes and they bear with them the banner that proclaims them neither trespassers nor bandits in the gardens. The porters come down and speak to them and they offer gifts of perfume and dyes for the master as is the custom for travelers from a distant garth and the door is opened and they are led inside. I follow at the porter's command and I bear their bags into the upper chambers and bring them water to wash with and clean towels. And they say to one another, what an odd sort of beast is this and what is it called. And I say I am a claywife. They are from a distant land which does not have such arts they say as to make a servant of the dirt. But how ugly it is they remark to the porters and, we heard the lords of Asternal prized beauty above all other things.

It is so the porter replies but the rude earth can only be shaped so far and the potters make them in haste. For they do not last and this one is old and soon to be thrown away anyway. Are they good for sport ask the travelers. No says the porter, for they cannot fight. They only fetch and carry and do other simple things. They cannot even remember anything unless they mutter it to themselves constantly. This one does not mutter a traveler says and the porter replies, you have given it nothing to do. Go, claywife and see if your master will condescend to greet us the traveler instructs, and I go. Condescend to greet you condescend to greet you condescend to greet you I mutter. And I go.

The upper chambers of the garth are marble and porphyry and silver and lit with hain and brazeglass and here the master forbids anything which is not most pleasing to his eyes and ears and touch. Great portraits of his fathers all adorn the walls and scenes of the wars they fought before the garths were cut across the rivers and the hills. Long polished swords hang beside busts of the enemies they cut down and his musicians play high ornate music in the afternoons and the scent of the flowers of the garth are carried through the rooms by the western breezes. As is his custom the master is at the furthest end of the hallway and I bow as I enter.

The master is displeased to see me for I am ugly to him and I am rarely wanted in the upper halls. He demands to know why I have come and I say travelers from far away have come and ask that you condescend to meet with them. He beckons over his page and hands him a dagger and instructs him to punish the porter who allowed me upstairs but not so badly he cannot work by tomorrow. Then he sends me down and he follows soon after. By his mild response I think he is pleased to have noble guests since rarely do visitors grace his modest gardens with their presence. And he sends me with word to the kitchen that they should prepare a fine meal for midafternoon with spiced wine and fresh bloody meats. I repeat these words to myself as I go down the stairs but the secret tongue inside my head is naming the things I can take to my daughter in the lamp-house.

The guests praise all the food the servants lay before them, tasting each and every dish. So pleasant the gardens of Asternal they say as they peck and nibble, and we have been offered every amenity on our journey. We have had to carry no provisions ourselves and even now can barely eat. But the master insists they try more delicacies of his kitchen for he must show even to foreigners that his taste is impeccable and they dutifully sample each one. Their smiles are all alike bright and fixed and they praise the craftsmanship of everything that they see and the master is pleased more than I have seen in a long time. He is so pleased he indulges their whim to summon me and answers their questions on how I am made and when they complain that I am old and ugly he laughs and laughs and says yes it is so, would you like to see it destroyed.

And they ask if claywives give good sport when they are broken up and the master says never no and they say that that is a pity but yes perhaps after luncheon they would be delighted to see me destroyed and the master says let it be done. And then he sends me to bring them more fresh meat and spiced wine and I do. The cook has left a long sharp knife on the board next to the meat and when I set it down before one of the travelers I let it slide off. It nicks him in the arm and he is furious and says well you will be happy to be rid of this one. His smile does not change at all and when I look down at his arm there is a little trickle of glittering blood.

I return to standing quietly behind the master where he need not look directly at me. The master makes brief but polite enquiry after their business which is far away in another country. A priceless jewel was stolen from them and they wish to deal cruelly with the thief. The travelers ask many questions about the master's gardens which pleases him and he tells the stories of how the lowlands were conquered. He talks of the cities that were razed and the barbarians that his fathers helped to drive off the land, whose descendants are now the wild men of the woods. He calls for a servant to bring in his beloved hounds so he may show them to the travelers, the great beasts with the long bright teeth and the golden fur who will pursue the scent of blood as far as their legs can carry them he says. In the gardens he says there is good hunting but he prefers the hills for the wild men are a greater challenge than any other animal and their flesh as sweet. And the travelers laugh and titter and the master asks them how they amuse themselves in their country, what do they call it.

And I mutter quietly to myself, Carantu Carantu.

Carantu was it, the master asks. And then the travelers fall silent and the smiles disappear. And their faces change in a way I have never seen faces change before and they are like masks all the same and yet I feel for the first time I am seeing their true faces. Like and unlike my daughter. The face of my daughter is fair. These faces are empty and cruel. The travelers stand and I turn and run. When my feet hit the top of the steps I hear my master's body strike the floor. I hear a servant scream and then another and then I do not hear anything at all. I go straight for the lamp-house. I do not think I have much time.

I enter and my daughter is already halfway to her feet and she is afraid because she has heard the shouting. She understands as soon as she sees me. I take her up in my arms. She is lighter than most of the loads I carry. When I reach the door I see one of the hunters at the entrance to the chambers. He is kneeling down next to a hound holding what looks like a broken dart still bright with blood. I turn for the door, the eastern door that leads out of the garth, out of all the garths to the places where I have never gone. To the wilderness. And I run as fast as I can with my daughter in my arms.

My clay is beginning to crack and my daughter is weak when we stop. It is near sunset again and great Edjumar is high in the sky. He shines through the treetops down at us and I lay my daughter down on the soft moss beside a riverbank. Her eyes are filled with his light and the light of his brothers the stars. We have not heard the baying of hounds in many hours. But my daughter's face is pale and the secret tongue inside my head is speaking terrible words.

I say I have little time left but she must find the strength to keep going. I do not know what to do now. My clay is cracking I say and I cannot go on much further. She shakes her head. You can she says you can, and not alone. And I say I do not understand. But in truth I am beginning to and I am afraid.

And she takes my hand and she says I have given her a wonderful gift and she will give me one in return. And she takes a chip of stone and she carves strange letters into my clay and she sings softly a song I have never heard before, high and unhappy to my ears. But I feel something change in my clay and the strength return to my limbs. A strength I sense will not soon desert me. Because of you I will see the face of my daughter she says and I will know she is safe and far far away. Take her far from Carantu and far from Asternal and I say, I will.

Soon she is giving birth. And soon after that she is gone. And O my granddaughter now I hold you in my arms and we are going, we are going long miles away. But know this in your sorrow and in mine, that your mother held you in her arms and beheld your shining face before she died. And she has given us both a mighty gift, for we are free we are free we are free.

VULTURE BEES TRANSFIGURE THE MAN I TRIED TO BE

RICK HOLLON

see: tender, suspended at the tip
of arm hairs that never darkened
    never hearkened or grew
the tangle of my father's muscle
the way he mangled through skin
    under thin bindings, not yet bone:

a bicycle wheel, unsteady ecliptic
starsign, phenotypically confined
    stars divined in blue, in old
time guidebooks, colorless water-fed
slender spine and narrow hipped, I
    was rendered, engendered, yet:

vulture bees sensitive, uncertain
plumose tender my roadside carrion
    ferry onward, yellow coinweight
bees pinned in lashes, my delicate hairs
catalyzed the old old instinct to feed
    thin-winged distinctions of queens:

conferred in me to me, bee-fed
on royal jelly, on rest stop tables
    carved through ribs, punched holes
I swallowed, vulture bees enveloped
my stomach, my outline, incorporeal
    incorporated—my hive hummed:

belly alive with foot tips, with comb
engorged I breathed bee vultures
    breathed cultures in mediums
ghostwise honeycomb in waxed
arteries, jelly slicked and sucked
    jelly licked and fucked I become:

wings split my skin up my middle
seams my father mapped, outlines
    of scenes, what seemed to be, the me
from which he wouldn't permit to deviate
the bauplan, the grand boyplan of his genes
    deviously unmarked, unmarred, unsnarled:

all categories of caution and confinement
of contempt, contemporary mores against
    all my stores of queenly drops, my coins
golden stops along the fairywise bees
path of roadside meadow, roadkill sweet
    honeyed meat of what I couldn't have been

YOUR FIRST DAYS BACK IN THE COURT OF ARTHUR

ABIGAIL ELIZA

YOU REMEMBER WHEN you used to love him.

You remember how this time a year ago, you did not hesitate before the thought, *I will die for him if only he asks*. And he asked. He did. He asked you before anyone. And it did not matter that the order was cruel, because it was Arthur who gave it, and how could he ever be something other than your light? You earned your title for him, *best of all knights*. You counted each point of your pentangle on his fingers. You did it so he would look at you a little longer. And he did. He does. He looked at you before anyone. He asked you first. This is your oath. You did not think twice before swearing it. *My sword, my life. Bravest, best. For you. For you.*

Last Christmas a green knight offered Arthur a game of equal exchange: strike him anywhere, and receive the same in return. He came with a great axe across one arm, a holly branch in the other. Arthur was so caught up in himself that he did not understand the offer also extended to the branch: there was a way out that didn't require a fight. You were so caught up in Arthur that you cut off the knight's head when you were asked. *If you strike the right blow*, Arthur had murmured, near to your mouth, *he will not be able to issue one in return.* It was a clear order. You're good at orders. He was close enough you felt his heat. He was close enough you held his light.

So when the knight rose and picked his head up off the ground, it seemed only natural that you'd die. You'd said you would and you meant it. You remember how you used to love him. And yet you were given a year: settle your affairs, make Arthur love you, seek out the Green Chapel, get what you are owed. Blow-for-blow. Equal exchange. All you could think was how glad you were that it was you instead of him. *If only he asks.* He asked. He did.

A year passed. You did not make Arthur love you. You did not settle your affairs. It would always be unequal but that was the point of your life: a pentangle has an odd number of spokes. You left Arthur's court to get what you were owed, and you spent three days in the court of that green knight, and when you went to his Chapel and you knelt and you *didn't die*—

You came back ashamed, biting your tongue, stomach in your fists, back to Arthur's court, and you came back ashamed because you discovered, in the end, that you did want to live. *You did want to live.* You wanted more than that: the pelt of a fox, the still-beating heart of a boar. A kiss you did not have to beg for. A kiss where you understood, clearly, from the start, what you were giving and what you could expect in return. Fair odds never seem a miracle until you remember what the rest of the world will offer.

Aren't you happy? You came back to Arthur, light-bringer. You should be happy. You told the knight you couldn't stay. You told him you had built a place where you could be proud, but of course by *proud* you meant a place where everyone told you that you were doing the right thing. A place where you didn't have to think. A place where you reflected the light. There's a lot to say for being a dog, for standing behind someone and swinging an axe when asked. There's a lot to say for bowing your head when the time comes: for trust, for a belt, for three kisses—two—one. There's a lot to say for when the knight took your face in his hands and your face was level with his hips. There's a lot to say for when the knight knelt down beside you and said, close, soft, *why is it you flinch?*

ORIGINALLY PUBLISHED IN *ASEPTIC AND FAINTLY SADISTIC: AN ANTHOLOGY OF HYSTERIA FICTION* (2023)

MOTHER MANSROT IN THE GLASS MOUNTAIN

SARAH PAULING

THERE WERE WALLS WITHIN the glass mountain, just as clear as its sheer cliffsides. There were floors within the glass mountain—and ceilings, too—but they left just as little to the imagination. A shining citadel of rooms; a pyramid stripped of secrets.

Even the palace, fit snugly at the mountain's heart, sat bare to the rest of us. The princess shed light like dandruff from the glinting gemstones of her dress. Four rooms below, my back aching and my hands cracked from the washing water, I would clutch my broom's handle and watch her petticoats trail.

When I first arrived, the mountain folk—for all our human filth and decay—seemed a relief to look upon. My eye caught on them through a hundred glass floors, a reprieve from transparency and light. But after years of watching—watching the royal huntsman slaughter deer in the crystal forest, watching the stableboy shit in the huntsman's stew, watching the blacksmith and the butcher breed—I grew restless.

My thoughts turned, again, to escape.

I was plucking peas for Old Rinkrank's supper when I first saw the youth outside the mountain.

He was a stocky thing, bred on corn and beef from the village. His broad shoulders made his pack look small. He ambled toward the mountain's base, eyes raised toward the distant princess as his hands floated to his lips—as his nails pinched the fragile skin to tug strips of it away.

I was gathering green vegetables in a ground-level harvest room, where the glass magnified the sunlight into a heat that dabbed sweat onto my papered skin.

When he saw me watching, he approached the cliffside between us. "Good afternoon, old mother," he said, voice sapped by the glass.

"I'm not your mother," I told him, "though they call me Mother Mansrot."

"Who does?"

"My master and his like." My knees protested as I gathered up my bucket and scissors. I turned to leave—if Rinkrank looked down from his rooms to see me dawdling, I'd sleep in the stables again.

"I'm here to save the princess," the youth said.

"Of course you are. Of course."

"But I'm smarter than the others were."

My breath caught. I whirled on him. "And why is that?" I stalked to the glass; pressed my fist to its surface. "You can climb sheer glass? Outsmart the great eagle and see past the trick mirrors? What do you have that a hundred men and... and all the others did not have?"

The youth's eyes widened. Then his abused lips edged into a smirk like we shared a secret.

"I'm a good listener," he said.

The mountain was no older than the princess. That's all anyone knew for sure.

When I was a young woman in the village, shy and strange in ways that rubbed up under my skin like a rash on backwards, I'd heard it said that a foreign king had protected his daughter by growing a wall of glass around her heart. He gave her dresses and soldiers and servants and commanded her not to age. He bid her to only wed whatever brave soul could pull her out of the mountain.

No matter what. No matter who.

I believed that once. Why else would I have come?

I'd cross the woods, again and again, to visit her: I'd picnic at the mountain's base, watching her pace her raised and inset quarters like a fox in a trap. Watching her freckles wax and wane with the seasons like the moon's reflection in water, just as my freckles did in the sun.

She never watched me back.

That night, because I knew him, I asked Rinkrank for whiskey.

His yellow teeth filled up my vision as he laughed in my face. "What does a hag need whiskey for? You'll stop your own heart."

"You're older than I am," I said, making my voice needy and plain. "You're frailer—"

His ring, when it hit my jaw, left a bruise shaped like a family seal. Rinkrank used to be someone, outside the mountain—I never learned who. Just that when he arrived, young and hearty, to save the princess, he'd thought they would be a good match by blood.

He grabbed a bottle from his cabinet, uncorking it with his teeth. He took a swig in front of me, swallowed, and belched.

I slunk to the kitchen, eyes watering with pain—the eyes of

the world on my back. The cook five rooms over leered; the children two above stared through their nursery floor until the nanny swept them away.

Getting Rinkrank to open the bottle was all that mattered. Because I knew him, I waited until he'd drunk himself to sleep, his knobby knees sharp under the moldering blanket on his rocking chair.

Then I slipped from his rooms, and—ignoring the gaze of the patrolwoman—went back to see the youth outside the mountain.

He was waiting for me beside the harvest room, hidden beyond off-season cornstalks. The mountain widened at the base, allowing for corners of privacy at its very edges. I sank to the ground slowly, letting dirt coat the knees of my dress.

"Tonight, you will go into the forest," I told him, "and hunt two predators: one beautiful, one strong."

The youth twisted a piece of skin on his lip, watching me. Blood pearled up beneath his nail.

"You will capture a mimic firefly, who pretends a mating dance until its victims are in reach. Find the one that flashes brightest—so bright your eyes water." I paused for breath, blunt anticipation pressing on my spine. "And you will kill a lynx. You will cut off its claws and fasten them to your own hands and feet."

"How?" he asked calmly.

"You'd better not be asking me how to kill, boy, or you'll never make it up the mountain—never mind down through its rooms after."

"How do I fasten the claws to my hands? Is that why you asked for rope?"

"Idiot." I pressed my fingertips to the glass between us.

Horror dawned alongside understanding as he saw the scars.

"She's been trapped here a long time," I told him. "Longer than you or I've been alive. Are you worthless or are you ruthless?" I crooked my fingers into claws. "The rope will get us out of here. Now shut up while I tell you what comes next."

There were mirrors in the mountain.

Sometimes suitors found ways to climb the sleek mountainside—clever ways or careful ways or bloody ways. But once they reached the crest, they found challenges they could not see from below: a deep gorge, and an eagle furious with hunger. Mirrors, indistinguishable from clear glass, disguised the danger until it was too late.

We'd learned this bitterly, those of us who survived. But I began to believe something else, too: there were secret mirrors at the mountain's heart.

The princess never left her chambers, where the glass was angled to bounce light from her skin and set her teeth to gleaming. Where all the world outside could see her dark hair and her rosy skin, her freckles thick as spots on a seashell.

Where she never ate or shit or bled.

How could she never leave? How could she *never leave?* How could she sit in an icy room with nothing in it but a four-poster bed and pace, and pace, and let the filth of the world watch her, and not want to smash through the glass with her own two hands? How could she not want to set her fists to bleeding?

How could she send her guard to reject us unfortunate survivors at the palace door?

Perhaps all the mountain had was her reflection, bouncing her beauty off every surface. Perhaps the mountain had an alluring hunger. Perhaps the mountain gently fed on us. There were more fireflies than lynxes in this world.

The youth didn't need to know that.

The following night, Rinkrank played cards with the neighbors. The stakes were high: he'd bet a room on the south side of his mean estate that adjoined both the knight's property and the priest's. Both wanted the space; Rinkrank wanted their coin.

My pulse sharp in my throat, I scrubbed the bedroom of his filth, watching through the walls. If they played late into the night, I'd miss the youth's ascent up the cliffside. I would not be there to remind him that the entrance "stairway" was just a trick of mirrors—that he must fasten his rope above the landing if either of us were to leave this place again. Young people were always stupid. I could leave nothing to chance.

Once, in my early mountain years, I'd thought to win myself a room in a card game. Property was the only kind of prestige recognized by the mountain folk. But Rinkrank would rather drown me in my own washing water than give me the satisfaction of any meager freedom, so I never did get to play.

When I was young, he used to stake me, playing against men who I'd seen watching me from their bedrooms. It was cold comfort that he'd never lost.

I waited while the men drank, while they gossiped, while they talked about who they'd last seen fucking. I waited until the moon had risen clear over the forest's canopy, and then I saw the youth climbing the mountain.

He pulled himself, claw over claw, up the cliff face. Rust-red blood trailed behind him, and I remembered how that same slickness had felt under my own palms. My breath caught when

I realized how quickly he moved, how smoothly. Hope, an unfamiliar vintage, twisted through me.

Others watched him, too: I saw the nanny place a bet with the butcher's boy. They did not warn him away.

The priest had a bad hand, and he left first, claiming an early service—a polite but useless lie, when everyone could see that his flock met after midday. The knight played to win: he and Rinkrank raised, and drank, and raised.

Finally, as the youth dwindled into a speck of darkness far above, the knight threw down his cards. Rinkrank howled with laughter as his neighbor stormed out the door. Then he called me in to clean their mess, stumbled to his rocking chair, and pulled his blanket tight around him.

As soon as his eyelids fell, I bolted for the door.

My first mistake.

"Where the hell are you going?" he murmured. I froze.

Then, louder: "Where the *hell* are you going?" He pulled himself to his feet, blanket catching between his shins and the footstool. "Answer me."

"To fetch the lantern lighter," I said, mouth dry. "The—the lights burn too bright for sleeping. I thought—"

He shoved me. My ankle twisted. I fell to the floor and caught myself by the palms. Pain cracked up my arms; settled into my shoulders. He planted his boot on my back and pushed me the rest of the way down.

"I hear you've been walking out on me, Mother Mansrot." The words wandered drunk on his tongue.

My saliva smeared on the floor. Through it, the patrolwoman watched me from the room below. She tipped her hat to Rinkrank.

"*You,*" I mouthed. "*I'll kill you.*"

The woman shook her head and walked on. Maybe it wasn't her that exposed me—it might have been the priest, or the nanny, or her children. It didn't matter.

Rinkrank heaved his weight down on top of me. I felt a *crack*, and screamed.

His reflection grinned in my saliva. "You know better than this —you know me better. You and me, we're trapped until the end of us."

He hooked his arms under mine, dragging me upward— dropped me in his rocking chair. He twisted his ring on his hand. "Everyone will see this," he said. "They'll know I don't take lip from anyone."

The round shape of an empty bottle pressed between my thigh and the armrest.

Rinkrank closed his hand to a fist. "They already know what *you* are." He braced the other hand against the headrest. "They know you're an *unnatural* woman who'll scrape and die and decay down here with the rest of us." He pulled back to strike.

My hand closed on the bottle's neck. I smashed it into the side of his head, barely hard enough to break—he staggered sideways. I tackled him to the ground. Shoved the sharp end into his eye.

He screamed, cursed, threw me off—I rolled, grabbed a stray shard, then dragged myself to my knees over him again.

Because I knew him, I sliced his neck from end to end, a grinning gash that slobbered blood on the floor in an even pool. A carpet of red—opaque. A meager protection from eyes below.

I sat back on my haunches, gasping for breath like a woman half-drowned. Every inhale burned. Rinkrank was far from beloved, but eventually someone would send a runner to alert the palace guard—if the patrolwoman, a dark uniform in the distance, did not already see.

My chest screaming, my lip bleeding, I limped for the still-open door.

As a girl in the village, I did not think to climb the mountain for a long time. I was used to watching women who did not look my way.

The princess wore beautiful dresses that flared at her waist, all lace embroidery and silk brocade. Sometimes, if I was very lucky, I would arrive at the mountain's base in time to see her brush her hair—as thick and dark as mine was.

I believed myself content. After starving for long enough, you can convince yourself that *seeing* and *feasting* are the same.

I left Rinkrank's blood in handprints as I staggered against clear stairwells.

The youth was nearly at the crest. Mountain folk watched me from their bedrooms and their servants' quarters, their kitchens and their outhouses. Some looked frightened. Some looked sorry. No one stopped me. No guardsman gave chase.

I dragged myself up and up, room to room, staircase to staircase, until I was level with the bottom of the clear gorge. I saw the bodies, flesh sloughed off faces as they decayed in open air. There was the skinny ginger with the limp, pierced through by the gorge's crystal spikes. Then there was the foreign lad, disemboweled by the eagle's giant beak. He had listened more closely than most, and his lynx claws were still secure, visible against shriveled hands trapped and eaten away by time.

Some good it had done him. Some good they'd all done me.

I was three rooms below the surface when the great eagle attacked the youth.

It turned imperious circles above him, then let loose a diving cry. The youth remembered my instructions: he grabbed onto the eagle's claws and held firm. The bird pulled him up—over the gorge. It struggled to throw him, higher with every frantic wing-beat. The youth's thick legs dangled far above me. He didn't let go.

The texture of pain in my chest sweetened and sharpened until I couldn't tell it from hope. Maybe—finally—this one was different.

I reached the highest room. Instead of a ceiling, there was a chute, deeper and sheerer than any stone well. I'd fallen down it myself, years ago—convinced I was seeing stairs.

The youth raised his hand to the eagle—the eagle screamed and released him. He fell down to the mountain's surface beside the chute, a showering of blood droplets around him.

"Hurry!" I called. "The rope."

The youth tied the rope's end to the post at the entryway, then dropped the rest down to me—I touched the hemp with an elation edging on pain.

He slid down the rope to meet me, landing tenderly on one bare foot. "Where is she?" His breath came hard. "Take me to her."

"I got you this far. I'm going to the surface."

He grabbed my wrist with a clawed hand. Blood dribbled from the gashed skin at his fingertips, his palm sticky-wet against my skin.

I looked at him. Darker blood rolled down his forehead. It pooled in the rips and crevices of his lips.

"Did you do as I said?" I asked him. "To the eagle?"

"What does it matter?"

"The—the firefly. You used it? You used its flare to daze him?"

He shook his head. "I found a quicker way. I used my claws to rend his." He curled his fingers against my wrist, sharp points into skin until skin gave beneath them.

It hurt—it all hurt—but I should have seen it coming. The stories we told ourselves in the mountain never survived contact with other people.

"You idiot!" I gasped. "The eagle is the only way across the gorge! You've trapped us both here."

The youth's mouth went slack. "But—but I brought the rope—"

"The rope doesn't matter if we can't cross the gorge!" I beat uselessly at his shoulder. "You've doomed us both, and for what? A pretty ghost?"

"She's more than that."

"She's not *real!* She's a reflection! You look at her and see yourself! The guard will never let you *near* her."

The youth closed his bitten lips. His face turned white.

Then he wrapped a strong arm around my neck and dragged my back to his chest. Pain flared through my ribs.

"I'll *make* her see me," he murmured in my ear. "I don't care if she's not real. I'll make her crown me."

"Why would she?" I wheezed. "You're nothing down here. You're both nothing. You're a body, she's a shadow."

He pushed his claws into the flesh of my neck. They felt like nettle stings. "I was nothing anywhere else, either. I can be worthless, or I can be ruthless."

I laughed, shaking with it. "You think I'm a hostage. Idiot boy."

"I'm stronger than you."

"Do you see the guard? Do you see anyone coming to stop you?"

His body stilled. He listened.

"There's no one," I said. "I thought they'd stop me, but—but when everyone can see you, there's nowhere to run. They can wait you out, understand? Predators that hunt at a goddamn walking pace."

"They'll come," he said, tightening his hold. "They'll come, and I'll make them—"

"I'm nobody," I said. "You could kill me right now."

The youth's claws trembled. Warm blood—or sweat, or saline—dripped from his chin and splattered against my neck.

His next breath came gasping, and he pushed me away. I fell against the wall.

"I'll cross the gorge myself," he said. "I'll—I'll claw myself down the side and weave through the spikes. I'll fight off the eagle."

"You'd be alone. You can't carry her with you."

He didn't answer.

I coughed up a glob of blood. Pressing myself to the wall, I made for the door—deeper into the mountain.

At the doorway, I looked back. Tears tangled in the youth's thick eyelashes. He gazed up through the chute—watched stars flicker like fireflies. I left him that way: one hopeful hand on the rope. The other tearing skin from his lip.

I dragged myself back through rooms and rooms. Twice I fell. Twice I stood up again. I made for the mountain's heart.

I saw the patrolwoman waiting for me in a room that lay outside the palace wall. Her eyes moved from Rinkrank's blood on my palms to my silver hair to my desperate limp.

"Killed your master and ran," she said. "You must have really thought this one would make it. Was he special? Or are you running out of time?"

Her own hair was a dark chestnut, as mine had once been, only graying around the temples. Her father was a patrolman, and his mother before him—maybe stretching back as far in time as the enigma of the mountain did. She served the princess at its heart.

She wore a string of lynx claws around her neck.

Though her empty room was no larger than Rinkrank's kitchen, I did not attempt to cross. Instead, I sank down at the glimmering wall, where I could watch the princess pace her chambers.

My eyes darted to the patrolwoman, my breath coming in fits and starts. The lines of her brow softened. She inclined her head.

The starlight played like fireflies in the princess's eyes. Her fingers were long and delicate; her lips like rosebuds waiting for the chance to bloom. She gazed, unfocused, at a point beyond my shoulder.

"What are you?" I asked her—asked the freckles on her collarbone. "What *were* you?"

She made no answer.

"Damn you!" I lunged for the glass; pounded it with shaking fists. "What do you *want from me?*"

The patrolwoman's hand went to her pommel.

"I've tried to win you, I've tried to escape you, I—I've tried helping others." I blinked tears down my cheeks. "What do you want from us? From any of us?"

A sharp breath escaped the patrolwoman. She took a step forward.

I turned on her, half-rising only to fall again. "What is she? Tell me what she is or I'll fight you all the way to the guardhouse and every minute after. Even if it's the last thing I know, I want to *know*. Was she ever real?"

"It doesn't matter."

"It matters! It matters more than anything!"

The patrolwoman's grip on her pommel turned protective—uncertain.

Quietly she said, "There are no stories in the mountain—no secrets. I'm offering you this small ignorance. Don't you want to take it?"

I scrubbed the blood from my lips, my wrinkled hands like sand rubbing skin. Darkness rose and fell like a tide at the edge of my vision.

The patrolwoman said, "You could decide she was a person once. That she escaped. Ran. That the mountain trapped her reflection as its lure."

The princess looked right through us. Or perhaps she looked through every wall, through every mirror, through every foul and fleshy body to the dark and open sky.

"Then I'll follow her out," I said. "This isn't the end of us." I spat blood on the crystal wall.

The patrolwoman's hand landed heavy on my shoulder. She pulled me to my feet. Silent and thoughtful, she led me away, half-carrying my weight.

And all the mountain watched: a sight that left us hungry, and a hunger that saw.

EAT IT OUT

CYPHER

I unzip you from cave mouth
to sex-craved stomach, spilling
your brown flesh coat
to the sides. I'm eye to eye
with your teenage
thoughts, each stored safe
on the shelves of your ribs. I run

my fingers along the bones
of bunched-up underwear,
an old shower head, and a Playboy
magazine. To the left, there's the handle
of a hairbrush, wet
with the smell of sex. Your body is overrun
by a cascading pink flush. I stick my head
into your open chest, and confess:
If it makes you feel better, my first dick
was a bottle of whiteboard eraser fluid.

Your laugh drips down my head, rubbing
the tender spot behind my ears. It's funny
how we stored our first meetings
with shame in similar ways. I remove
my hands from you, and rip myself open—
belly button to salivating pussy. I see you

see the stash of gay comics, the desperate
self-convincing that this was mere curiosity,
the small ghosts of girls I called close friends
but thought of kissing, and the stack of plaid
t-shirts I tucked into capri pants
all through ninth grade. Your teeth
toy at my insides, eyes still locked on mine,
as you eat my teenage shame out.

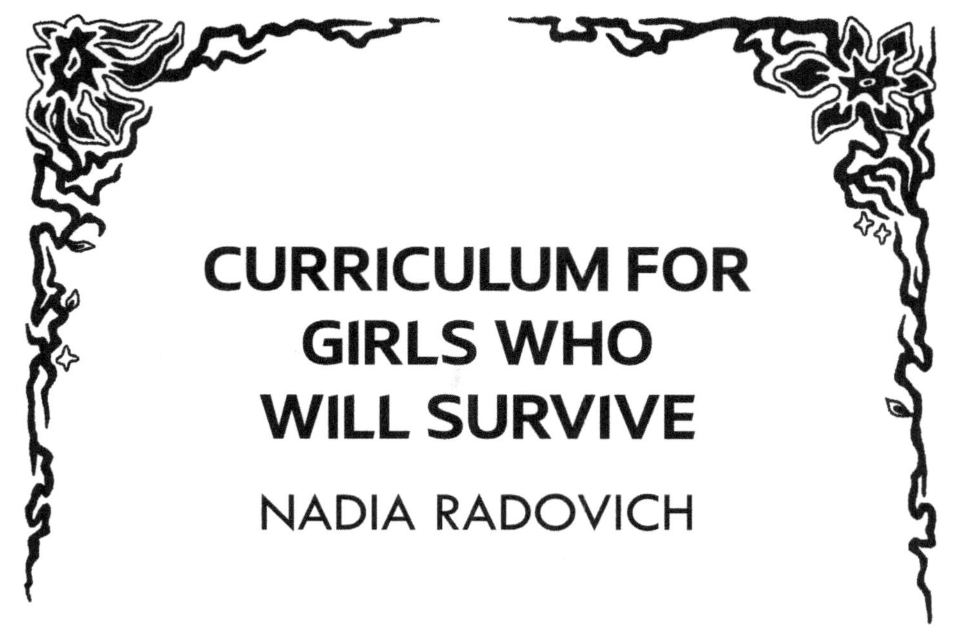

CURRICULUM FOR GIRLS WHO WILL SURVIVE

NADIA RADOVICH

I. Animal Husbandry

THE DAY YOUR MOMS become infected, you're in your animal husbandry class, taught in the tack room of the barn. Sarah's mom is holding up a chicken egg, saying, "Eggs are valuable, versatile, and portable. You can eat 'em, trade 'em for ammo, or grow 'em into more chickens, just as long as you *pay attention when I'm talking, Kitty.*"

"I'm listening, ma'am," you say automatically. She squints like she's not so sure. But you're the leader's daughter, so she lets it slide.

You weren't listening. You were thinking how your mom's favorite mare is pregnant, which is the biggest thing to happen ever. Southern Green has chickens, milk cattle, Nubian goats, and four extremely good mares, but it's never had a foal before. Sure, sometimes your mom calls you *my little filly*, but it's not the same.

"As I was *saying*," Sarah's mom continues, "eggs have a bloom on the outside of the shell that keeps the bacteria out. It's why we don't have to refrigerate eggs until we wash them," and you slip back into thinking about yourself as a tiny filly racing around Southern Green. You wonder if your mom's gonna give you the baby horse, like a horsey little sister, and you're lost in anticipation up to your eyeballs when Sarah says, "Mommy, you all right?" and something about her tone pulls you out of it. She sounds funny. If it were Stephanie sounding like that, you wouldn't've thought twice. But this is Sarah, who's not scared of anything.

"Fine, girls," Sarah's mom says, but she doesn't look it. "I—I had a turn just there. But I'm all right, I'm—"

You've read a phrase in books, where someone turns white. Sarah's mom has turned grey. No, not grey: silver, like the canned sardines your mom traded ammo for once. It would be beautiful if you'd never seen a person turn that color before.

"Girls, you looking at this?" Sarah's mom says, but she's not talking about her skin. She points just behind you at the blank wall, the closed door. She looks at it like there's something there. Like she's devouring the world with her eyes. "Jaysus, that's beautiful." Her voice rattles. "Girls, you seeing this?"

And the worst part is, you think you're starting to. Something is happening to the light. It's still bright, but it's turning grey somehow. Your mom taught you that this is what X-rays looked like, like light itself was turning inside out.

She said this a lot. It was important to remember, she said. It was how you recognized the infected.

You're not supposed to look at them, ever. That's how it spreads. But you can't look away from Sarah's mom. It's like she's a black hole. All the light is bending toward her. Your hair is rising off your shoulders and streaming toward her. Your vision is turning out and out and out. It *is* kinda beautiful.

There's a flat sound. You blink, and the room is normal again.

You're still at your desk, but Stephanie is on her feet. She's picked up the tack room shovel. *Stephanie.* Stephanie, who hates the infected, and darkness, and food that isn't brown. Stephanie, who's good with chickens, who's the only one who doesn't complain when she gets assigned to cleaning the chicken shit off fresh eggs because she says she likes the chance to think and likes the texture of the smooth, round, hard, fragile, warm eggs.

Your brain keeps offering up all these little details to drown out the sound as Stephanie lifts the shovel again. This time it comes down wet.

II. Hand-to-Hand Combat

The thing is, as you let Stephanie haul you to your feet, as she shoves you and Sarah toward the door, it feels like you've forgotten all your lines. Like you're the one—the leader's daughter, the loud-mouthed, laughing one—who's supposed to say, "We need to get to the barn, now," and then, "Can you grab Sarah and pull her along? I think she's in shock—"

But it's Stephanie. Stephanie, who makes you slip unwashed eggs into your pockets, fill your bottles with water. She makes you grab your shotgun.

She hustles you toward the stalls. But then she stops, so fast you walk into her. Stephanie's mom is there. She must have been loading cartons of eggs into the wagon, before she'd have dusted off her hands to come teach your next class.

The cartons are open now; she's holding the eggs in her silver hands. You watch her drop one. It cracks in a pool of spreading yellow. You'd've been switched for dropping an egg.

"Girls, you seeing this?" Stephanie's mom says, staring in fascination at the wetness that was formerly an egg. "If that ain't the most beautiful thing you've ever seen—"

You slip your hand around Sarah's elbow.

"This way," you whisper, tugging her toward the far stall. It's your mom's mare, sorrel sides swelling with a baby, wider and wider with each big breath. Your mom left her halter on; it's the work of a moment to hook on a lead rope. Sarah's bare foot is dusty and cool when you coax her into stepping into the stirrup of your hand, sliding up bareback behind the mare's withers.

Stephanie's still standing in the aisle, staring at her mom.

You want to say something. Your mind has gone as dry as an overused well.

"We gotta go," is all you can think of, and Stephanie nods. Making up her mind about something. Then y'all are running out of Southern Green, mare trotting, Sarah bouncing, Stephanie's mother still crying, "Girls? Girls, you seeing this?"

III. Horsemanship

You stumble out the gates of Southern Green, three girls on one horse. Two horses, really. Your mom told you it was safe to ride a pregnant horse. She laughed when you asked and said, "After all, I was pregnant with you when I first escaped the infected."

It's true. It's how your moms met, yours and Sarah's and Stephanie's. They were in a Lamaze class together, up in the city on the first day of the plague. They drove out into the country together, and when the truck ran out of gas, your mom rustled up some horses and led them to her grandpa's farm, Southern Green.

They were an unlikely trio. Stephanie's mom, a karate instructor. Sarah's mom, former 4-H kid turned stay-at-home mom, gardening and canning queen. Your mom, a stable brat who grew up hunting deer with her grandpa.

You wondered if they knew how important those skills would be. Maybe it would've been cool to be hardened soldiers with machine guns at first, but they would have starved as soon as they made it to the farm. Knowing how to clean an egg without giving yourself salmonella ended up being more important than automatic weapons in the end. Stuff like that was how you survived.

You've never really thought about this before. But you think your moms must have. Otherwise why would they have spent so much time teaching you?

"We should head for the cave on the rise," Stephanie says. She's back to business, lead rope in hand. "Where we used to camp."

She's talking like she's been thinking this whole time and decided this is the best thing to do. You don't know how she's doing it. Your head is still full of the sound brain makes when it meets shovel.

"I want to go home," Sarah says. It's the first thing she's said since you left her infected mom in the classroom.

You can't think of anything to say, so you just slip your hand into hers, and she squeezes it. Stephanie is walking ahead, pointing out holes in the trail, so Sarah can nudge the horse aside with her knee. You're glad she's taken charge. You're torn between feeling relieved, and feeling like, if the infected are still capable of opinions, your mom would be let down.

You realize with a jolt that it's the first time you've thought of your mom as infected.

Your moms used to take you camping in this cave, a sort of end-of-semester test. Once she checks to confirm it's empty, Stephanie finally lets Sarah slide off the horse.

"We're gonna need a fire," Stephanie says.

"I've got it," Sarah says unexpectedly. "Not a whole lotta wood left." But she obediently picks up the pieces you left the last time you camped, takes them out front so you don't asphyxiate from the smoke.

Stephanie untacks the horse. She doesn't tell you to do anything. Maybe she thinks that'd be weird, too.

"God*damn*," Stephanie says, so sudden you jump. She sounds like she's gonna cry. "God*damn* but I didn't bring a frying pan. I'm so *stupid*, how are we gonna cook the eggs?"

Your mouth is moving before you can think, the way it always does.

"Check your pockets," you say. "Someone's gotta have a fruit leather or protein bar or something that came out of a wrapper." It's a treat your moms give you sometimes, when the hens have been laying well and there's plenty to trade.

You find it in the pocket of Sarah's jacket, an empty foil shell that once held gummy snacks. What you don't say is, cooking eggs in foil's a trick that only works a couple times. It means you're gonna have to decide what to do next, sooner or later.

IV. Agriculture

You shouldn't be able to sleep, curled up on the ground with Sarah at your back and Stephanie on watch. But you must manage it somehow, because you keep having the same dream, over and over. Each time, it jerks you awake like a fish on a hook, then swims back as soon as you close your eyes.

You dream you're in the little hallway off your mom's bedroom in Southern Green. The door's open a crack. You're standing in front of it, listening to your mom move inside. You can hear her brushing her hair.

You don't get a lot of time with your mom. She doesn't belong to you: she belongs to Southern Green. You're just one of the five people she has to take care of.

You want more than anything to open the door, to sit on the bed beside your mom. There's something you've gotta ask her. It feels like things will work out okay if you can just get inside. But it's a dream. You can't even raise your hand to the door.

You wake up with a hand on your shoulder and water on your face. It's Stephanie. She's crying so bad the tears are running into her hair. She keeps saying your name over and over, so hard it's like her teeth are chattering.

You're scared she's gonna wake Sarah, so you take her outside. You don't have a handkerchief, so you take your flannel off and try to get her to blow her nose in it. She's so out of it, it's like she's forgotten how.

"What is it?" you say. Your throat hurts. It feels like you're still dreaming.

Stephanie sucks in a deep enough breath to say, "I don't know what to *do*," and it sets her off crying again.

You're scared she's gonna spook the horse, so you make her sit on the ground. You crouch beside her, put your hand on the back of her neck and make all the soft sounds you make with your teeth to calm a horse. Shushing her until her breathing evens out. It's easier that way. It saves you from having to think of something to say.

"We didn't—we didn't bring any grain for the horse," Stephanie manages to say. "We didn't bring any ammo, Kitty. We didn't bring *anything*. We've only got enough water for two days, then we're gonna have to do something about it. But I keep turning it over in my head, and *I don't know what*. I don't know what to do, I don't know what to do, I don't..."

"You need to sleep," you say, because you can't think of anything else. "I'll take watch." A moment later, you're not sure why you said it. It's not like things are gonna be better in the morning.

V. Home Economics

Sarah goes on sleeping. Stephanie lies down; you can hear her snuffling. You don't know if she sleeps. You sit on the ground next to the horse, listening to her nighttime breathing sounds, turning over what Stephanie said. Over and over as the sky lightens, trying to figure it out.

Your whole life, you woke up when it was still dark out. You ate the food you grew and did whatever tasks your moms gave you. Peeling potatoes, saving a few to bury again someday. Cutting the heads off chickens, eating them down to the gizzards and trading the feathers. Checking the thermometer *again and again* to make sure you quickened an egg and didn't kill it.

Some years it worked, and you got gummy candy, vintage MREs, hand-me-down blue jeans. Other years it didn't, and you learned how to sip hot water to stretch out food, and each time you wanted to cry about it, you couldn't, because your moms took food off their plates and put it onto yours.

You watch the sky lighten and wish they'd infected you, too.

Stephanie's back to normal when she gets up. She nods to you like you're her deputy, the same way her mom is deputy to yours. She cooks some eggs in the fruit leather wrapper. You don't know if the wrapper survived the cooking. You don't see it after, so probably not.

"Here's how I see it," Stephanie says, while the three of you eat overcooked eggs with your fingers. "We can either go somewhere else and figure out how to survive there. Or we can try to take back Southern Green."

You think about the other settlements, the ones your moms take turns driving the wagon to along the abandoned highway. You think what it would be like to ride a pregnant mare down shelled-out asphalt you've never seen, the burnt-out city spectral in the distance.

Then you think of Southern Green. Door frames carved with marks proving how much you've grown. Closet shelves lined with bottles of hydrogen peroxide, quilts your great-grandma made, clean Mason jars. You were born in the living room, a week after Sarah and Stephanie. Whatever it is that makes up the three of you is embedded in that house, that barn, like dirt in grout.

"We can't take three infected," you say. "Not by ourselves. We just can't."

"Two," Sarah says unexpectedly. It makes you jump. "Two infected."

"That's right," Stephanie says. "Only two. And I believe we can. Just think of it this way. This is probably how our moms felt, all the times they survived."

You don't discuss it more than that. It's Southern Green or the rest of the world. There's nothing more frightening than that, not even the infected.

VI. Shooting

At Southern Green, the only thing worth as much as fertilized eggs and pregnant horses is ammo. You didn't take any with you when you left. Only what's already in your shotguns.

Your gun has one shell. You know who it's for. You have to keep forgetting about it, or you can't do what you need to do.

The three of you come down the trail, Sarah riding the pregnant mare. You and Stephanie keep looking at each other and then away. You think she's gonna let it lie, but when you get to the gate, Stephanie turns to you.

"You see your shot, you take it," she says fiercely. "I mean it, Kitty. I'll kick your ass if you don't."

She could, too. Stephanie's always been better at hand-to-hand combat than you.

You find your mom where you knew you would, in the little hallway off her bedroom. On the north side, where it's cool year-round in the shadow of the myrtles.

Your mom is sitting on the edge of her bed, facing away from you. She's holding her hairbrush in one fish scale-silver hand. She's brushed all her hair out. It's lying in hanks on the braided rug like pillow down.

Your hands are sweating so badly you're afraid you'll drop your gun.

"So?" you ask her. You have to know, in the same way the infected have to see whatever they're looking at, like it's your last hope of salvation. "Tell me, since you're so smart. What am I supposed to do now?"

Your mom raises her head, turns it. You pretend her eyes are looking at you, not past. Not at whatever it is that only the infected see.

The light is turning inside-out, rushing toward you like a tunnel. You feel like one of the MREs your mom got for you when you were little. Like a reaction has occurred. Like something inside you is boiling.

You think you know the truth now: that none of you are as strong as your mothers. Not as quick on horseback nor as good of a shot. You don't have that terrible hunger clenched in your teeth that means you *will* survive. This is your Lamaze class, and you are gonna die.

Your mothers could do anything in the world except make you as strong as them because, paradoxically, you never had to be. They allowed your softness through their strength. Now all that's left is you, and you don't think it's gonna be enough this time.

Your mom's mouth tips open. For a split second, you're scared she's gonna say she's disappointed.

Oh, baby, your mom says, as the world feathers out in greys and silvers and all the colors no one's named yet. *You're the shotgun now.*

So you take the shot.

SITUATIONSHIP

SEOUNG KIM

YOU LOOK UP FROM your book, wearing a smile you've reserved for me. "Tired of studying?"

I take a seat beside you and sprawl out, my back against the table. "I hardly see the point."

The top of the library is a skylight that opens out into the stars. The view was nice for the first month or so, but soon I longed for even the gray skies of home. Above us, the spires of the cathedral where we meet for Mass once a week jut out from the center of the ship.

"Get off," you say, shoving at my shoulder, "you're on my notes."

I'm taller and stronger than you, and I don't budge. I close my eyes, grinning when I hear your annoyed huff.

"Aren't you worried about your future?"

I know you're bitter. You're a scholarship student and I'm a legacy admission. Your parents are nobodies on some backwater colony, and I'm the son of a general.

"Yeah," I say. I reach up and flick one of your dark curls out of your eyes.

"You're weird," you say, but you close your book and stand up anyways.

We end up in the conservatory, letting mango juice run down our chins and listening to the ship's engines hum. This time, it is nearly instantaneous—the fuselage catching fire, the ship evaporating around us. The garden, and you, dissolve into the endless dark.

This is always where the story ends.

Each cycle I beg you to stay with me a little longer: ignore your studies, come back to the dorms, explore the underbelly of the ship. You laugh and bat me away, talking about your grades, your career.

When we were both children, my father brought you to me as a companion, a role model to keep me from acting out. It worked some of the time—the rest of the time we became partners in crime, inseparable.

Now we're aboard the most prestigious school this side of the Milky Way, with all the sons of state and industry learning how to run the galaxy by inflicting their petty tyrannies on each other.

To everyone else, you are quiet and studious. We've been together long enough that I can tell when you're angry at the things people say to you. All that "credit to your race" shit. Your thin face goes blank. Later, when we're alone in an empty hangar, you fume.

You hate when I defend you, because you hate drawing attention to yourself, or you just don't want me to suffer by association. Goddamn martyr. Maybe this is why you don't say anything about the fact that I'm in love with you.

It's always easiest when it happens in the middle of the night. There's only a split second of fear and pain, and then I wake up again in the past.

This time, it happens more slowly. The gravity breaks down first, and then the oxygen. We have emergency suits, but we won't reach the next station fast enough. I sit beside you and hold your hand, feeling the life ebb out of you.

"Do you remember the last plague of Egypt?" you ask.

I never paid much attention in catechism class. "Locusts?"

"God sent his angel to take all of the nation's firstborn sons..." You lean your head against my shoulder and close your eyes, like you're falling asleep.

This is where the story ends. Can we try again?

We're stopped to refuel. News comes in about the war. The other boys gather excitedly in groups to discuss the latest development: an insurrection put down by the empire. Some of the students are leaving for the rest of the semester, recalled by worried families or summoned to serve at their fathers' sides.

"You should get off here," you tell me. "Go home to your family."

"Come with me," I say.

A shadow crosses your face. I know how you feel about my father. I won't abandon you, though. What if time keeps on going without you?

You don't press the issue.

I don't see you all afternoon. After dinner, I find you speaking with a girl from the kitchens. She has dark hair like you. There's a twinge in my gut. I go up to her and put on my most charming smile.

"Hullo. What's a pretty thing like you doing here?"

She flushes and ducks back into the kitchen.

You round on me, furious. "I hate when you do that."

"You know her?" I ask. "Is she from back home?"

"No. No." You shake your head, like you're waking up from a dream. "I just had a question about the menu."

We sprawl out on the floor of the dorms, where we've dragged our mattresses together.

"Do you remember when I broke that ceramic horse your father liked, and you took the blame for me so I wouldn't be sent away?" you ask.

"Yes," I say. "He grounded us both for a month anyways. What brought that up?"

"Nothing."

When I wake up in the middle of the night, the space beside me is empty.

I think a part of me has always known. In the maintenance hatch, your arm deep in the guts of the ship's control mechanisms, you apologize to me.

I know there is nothing I can say to stop you. Instead, I rest my head on your shoulder. Your hair tickles my cheek. "I forgive you."

You lean against me, withdrawing from the tangle of wire, and stroke the back of my neck like a dog.

"I'll do it for you," I say. "This time, you can go home."

You slip the wire cutters into my hand, unable to speak. I bend down to kiss you, because why not? You kiss back politely, obligingly, figuring, I suppose, it's the least you can do.

This is where the story ends: I send you out into the stars, alone.

ELECTROLYSIS

NICO SANTANA

Winter: my electric microwave
   room is turning me into jerky.
I lift the fleece sheets and
prick my finger on a barb
of lightning; I try on a slipper,
and static punctures my sole.
Back in bed, I watch the ceiling
rotate, my head growing lighter as
its precious saltwater evaporates,
escapes from my circuit of exit
wounds. Good food. Pure food.

A fish removed from its ocean
   then removed again for good
   measure. I struggle towards
the supercharged doorknob, pop
open the door, and the greedy city
burns its grey hand to grab me,
quick and easy sterilized meat
dry as a crackling wire, ready to be
chewed up and digested in its
urban tract of gutters—go ahead,

eat me. You severed me from my foreign
contaminants, and now I'm reduced
to a briny husk. I hope the taste of it
stings. I hope it swims up your throat.

THE HOMEOWNER'S BRIDE

AYIDA SHONIBAR

WOODEN WHEELS CRACK against the dirt road, warning me of the owner's approach. His journey up my hill is slow. The cart fights its way through the brambles and wildflowers that have made the path theirs in the four decades since he left.

After all this time, I didn't expect anybody would have the gall to breach my gates again.

Moonlight filters through hundreds of pupillary openings in my geometric jali windows as I train my gaze to the front entrance. The homeowner ties his bull to the gatepost, jostles the cracked sign with my name—*Shiuli House.*

The sound of my locks falling to his keys makes my thorns bristle. I hope he pricks himself on the thistles I send creeping toward my doorway, but he kicks them aside.

"Shabdhan." He extends his arm, and I realise with increasing ire that he's not alone. "Don't trip on these vines."

A woman clutches his elbow and stumbles off the luggage-loaded cart. Crimson fabric shrouds her dark hair. Her face, turned to take in the overgrown tree branches weaving through my stone façade, is painted prettily in the white and red dots of Bengali bridal shaj.

Not only does this man intend to take up residence within me, but he dares bring a second person along.

This place is all mine. All *me.*

"It's a little untended," he says. "Nobody's been here in almost half a century."

His assumptions, as ever, render him foolish. I'll make myself known soon enough.

His bride is young, barely in her forties. Mortality lingers at the hollow of her throat, in the shallow breaths escaping her parted lips. A darling doll. There's no gold jewellery adorning her neck, so the homeowner must not have married her for her family's riches. He needs something else from her.

"The house will fall into good shape with your domestic touch," he says. "We'll live comfortably enough."

Her mehndi-decorated fingers reach toward the petals blooming in a bitter charcoal shade along my unkempt garden. "Are these shiuli flowers? They're not white like the ones growing by the road."

He catches her waist when she bends to take a closer look, stopping her before she can nuzzle my blossoms. They reek of rotten flesh, of stale blood. The things that have fed them.

"They used to be white once," the homeowner says. "Don't touch them, Chhaya. They might be poisonous."

She unrolls two mattresses in the old bedroom. They lie separately, no chance of a wedding night even without my interference.

The yellowed tiles have warped over the years, uneven like teeth, strings of vegetation growing between them. I dig the sharp edges into the newlyweds' backs, holding them in my maw. I scrape branches against windows and howl nightmares into their sleep, filling them with visions of insects within skulls and mouths wrenched open in agony. They toss and turn till dawn, minds reeling with distasteful thoughts of mine in their not-quite marital beds.

The bride rises first. For a minute, I think I've triumphed, ruined her rest. A few more nights of this, and they'll lose their minds. Then I'll slip inside and bend the homeowner to my will. Force him to abandon my premises for good.

But she just washes her face and cleans her mouth, then changes into a salwar kameez, lights a small fire outside, and brews a pot of tea. Her husband wakes to a steaming cup of cha pressed into his hands.

To a scene of domestic bloody bliss.

She lathers shaving cream over his face. Her hands sweep a razor along his jaw, comb coconut oil into his white hair. When she's finished, he hangs a mirror on the front door and smirks at his pampered reflection.

As if this house was built for him to live in.

I slam a heavy bough into the door. It smashes, taking the mirror and his smug reflection with it. That'll leave a bruise— but it's worth it.

The bull startles awake, yanking against its restraints. The bride rushes to soothe it, hiding her own distress to murmur gentle words of comfort.

Meanwhile, her husband surveys my figure. His eyes rove over my untrimmed hedges, pausing on soil rendered barren by weeds, staring at cracks and wrinkles in my exterior. "We have much work to do."

He disappears with the cart and returns in the afternoon with an axe.

The curve of my hill shudders at the impact of his blade against a tetul tree trunk. A gash opens in the wood, my pain oozing out with the resin.

This arrogant cad. He knows I'm wicked; the time for subtleties is gone. I curl a root around his ankle, toppling him.

He curses and reaches for the axe. For a sexagenarian, his reflexes are quick. The cold iron embeds itself in my grip, prying me loose. He doesn't stop. Lifts the weapon and delivers blow after blow until my roots become splinters.

When he's done, he wipes his brow and turns to the fractured front door. "Chhaya," he calls, "help me tame this beast of a house into something habitable."

She takes the axe and begins on the next tree.

I watch them sullenly as I nurse my wounds.

During a break from chopping my wood, the bride serves her husband a thala of dal bhat in the yard. She draws his attention by saying demurely, "Shunun," asking him to listen instead of directly invoking his name the way he casually takes hers. "Perhaps this house is too far gone to be lived in."

My doorways creak ajar in interest, eavesdropping. I've terrorised this woman's fragile nerves to their breaking point; I want to witness her admitting it to him, urging him to pack up and leave.

"We've no other options," he replies gruffly. "You know they took everything in the city when my business went bankrupt. This old house is the only possession I have left."

I rankle at his insult, dark shiuli petals fluttering in a gale that isn't there. He can cut down my trees and discard my debris, but I'll be no possession of his.

Her eyes flit to my flowers before drifting back to him. "With the—the *state* it's in, I'm concerned we'll become overwhelmed—"

"Do you have somewhere else to go, Chhaya? Your parents passed and left you nothing. Nobody else will take you at your age, when you can't even bear them heirs. This house is your last resort, too."

She bows her head.

"Is it too much, this roof over your head? Do you not want what I'm providing for you? Won't you do your side of the work to make our home?"

"Yes. Of course, I will."

After the meal, she sweeps my dishevelled floors with a jharu, even as I blow more dirt in through the back door. She notices, sighs deeply—and keeps going. As if we're playing a game. Performing a dance. Her mouth twitches once, though surely not in a smile. A pout, maybe. She doesn't give in as easily as I expect her to. But I don't let up, either. I'd almost feel sorry for her, if I didn't want her and her husband out of here.

He naps while I chase her around this way. I toss him a nightmare or two, but my efforts are wasted on him when she's the one mopping my cobwebs and scrubbing my tiles: shaving me, combing me, in the same meticulous way she did her husband earlier that morning. I itch under her ministrations, scoured by the first touch of a human I've endured in a long time.

Her lips curve again.

When she boils water for her evening bath, my walls tingle in anticipation. Here comes a moment that will strip her bare, render her completely defenceless.

That's when I'll strike. And show her what I truly am.

The bathing room is a simple chamber, empty save for the bride, her bucket, and a narrow canal that drains to the outside.

And me.

She dips a mug into the water. I focus my consciousness into it, concentrating on the thrill of manoeuvring a person into submission, of them tossing their head back in horror and screaming.

Her fingers curl around the vessel to tip it forward. I slide over the rim with the warm liquid, sluicing over her face. Her skin is a deep bronze, tapered around her onyx lashes and soft over her flat nose. The contact throws me into frenzied excitement. I vibrate with it, dripping down her neck and submerging her in my terrible essence.

She gasps. She feels me, senses the rush of adrenaline I elicit from her body. Fight, flight, and fright war through pliant flesh that reacts to my fluid embrace. Her nipples pebble beneath my downpour. Her back arches.

Quickly, she spills another mug over herself. I have her in my thrall, draping myself over her trembling form. I gush down between her legs. She makes a sound in the back of her throat, free hand slapping against the wall to maintain her precarious balance.

A third mugful and she's begging for my mercy. "Please!"

I consume her, feel her muscles clench. Power surges through me. Her neck curves back, teeth bared in a grimace, a moan in her mouth. Just like I wanted.

"Oh, god," she prays, sliding to the floor.

But there are no gods in the room. Only me, the monster.

She should flee from the bathroom after what she's observed of me. Instead, she whispers into the darkness, "Will you reveal yourself? I want to know you."

The air between us thickens with confusion. Her confession upends me and sends me sprawling. The door bangs open, making her jump. She scrambles to pull her clothes on and creeps back into the bedroom.

Where her husband sleeps on his bedroll.

He would find my actions disgusting. I remember the familiar way he pulled her back from my shiuli flowers when they arrived. He would consider my touching his bride an atrocity, something to fight with everything he has.

But he cannot ruin me now. Not when this house is all he has left. This time, I'm indestructible.

If he wants me to leave her alone, he'll have to take her far away.

Chhaya, I breathe from the darkest corner of the house.

She hears me and looks up from her bucket of laundry. A flash of interest sharpens her expression, interrupting her monotonous task.

A sideways glance at her husband tells her he didn't hear me call her name. He has warned her several times: "Don't wander by yourself. Stay where I can protect you."

She bites her lip. Perhaps she's come to her senses in the light of day and developed a healthy fear, after all. Nobody should entertain the idea of pursuing an interaction with me. I'm *dangerous*. She needs to be *sheltered* from the likes of me.

"I'm going to hang these to dry," she tells her husband. But when she leaves the room, she climbs up the staircase instead, disappearing into my ominous mist.

She opens the door to a room that's been untouched for forty years. Before she was born, it belonged to another lady. A former bride. The aging wood of the jamb groans threateningly, ready to collapse upon Chhaya at the slightest provocation. She should leave. We both know it.

Dust billows under her advancing footsteps. I slide into its slipstream and reward her transgression with a caress of her ankle.

She hums. "There you are."

I drift higher, moving up her petticoat. Waiting for her to change her mind and retreat.

"What are you?" she asks breathlessly. "How do you make me feel these things?"

In the stillness of the uninhabited room, she looms excruciatingly clear. The perfume between her clavicles draws me closer, until I can taste each drop of moisture on her: the dampness of sweat at her temples, on her tongue, between her thighs.

"Oh, god," she says again, in some sort of twisted worship that cannot belong to me. "I can see what you're thinking."

I press into her, wanting for a second to show her more of me, and she shakes.

"Can you kiss?"

Her words still me. I've been here before—a kiss that leads to doom. I see them again, the rotting skull, blood washing down the drainage canal. A fleeting vision of a young woman with a sharp mouth and mischievous eyes hovers in the air. Memories that no longer exist.

I wipe them away, but Chhaya holds on.

"Who's that?"

She doesn't know what I am. If she did, she wouldn't ask me to kiss her.

Her keen gaze cuts through the haze in the room, falling on the fading portraits lining the wall. She touches one. "Is that her? Was she here before me?" Her fingers begin to quiver. "Did you—did you kill her?"

And here, finally, is the fear. It snakes between us like a venomous viper and turns the room fragile. The frame slips from its precarious fastening at her touch, crashing to the floor.

"Chhaya?" Her husband thunders up the stairs. "Are you up there?"

He skids into the room like a hero from the legends, axe raised to defend his bride. His eyes take her in—flushed face, swollen lips, dishevelled clothing—and narrow. "Is there someone in here with you?"

Now he knows what I can do to her if he stays in my house.

A rope of ivy bursts through the window, wrapping around the hilt of his axe. He wrenches it away, stumbling into his bride. One of my thorny plants drags against Chhaya's cheek.

Immediately, I retract the braided stems.

The homeowner's gaze swings between her and my receding attack. "What's this?"

Chhaya presses a palm to her wounded face, eyes luminous with shock, and leaves wordlessly. My dust flutters by her feet as I attempt to follow, before I quash it back down.

The owner doesn't depart so quickly. He patrols the room, stopping at the fallen frame. He picks it up.

The wave of anger that lashes out of me surprises us both. The sketch flies from his hands as I snatch it away and pull myself into the cloudiest corner of the room. But I'm not fast enough.

He sees me.

Not as I am now, but the way I used to be. Sharp mouth, mischievous eyes. Feminine figure and a voice like ghungur bells.

His expression clears, confusion vanishing.

I don't want him to perceive me that way. It isn't who I am anymore. My shape follows the blunt edges of the building and the slow rise of the hill it sits upon. I am the flowers that soaked up the blood draining from my body so many years ago, the tetul trees whose roots my remains were concealed under. I'm the house that won't surrender to him.

Yet the homeowner won't regard me as I am. He sees what he wants—his property.

"Don't come near my wife again," he says.

He might brandish an axe to keep me in line, but there's a boundary even he won't cross. He cannot cut down my structure nor tear down my walls. Without me, he'll have nowhere to live. He can't overpower me in my true form.

I remind him of this by slamming my doors.

His jaw tightens. He moves to the window to peer down at the yard, where Chhaya hangs the wet laundry.

"I should think twice before burning you to the ground," her husband concedes. "But I can do anything I want to *her*."

It shouldn't matter.

My gaze bores bitterly into her back. From the moment I first saw her, I intended to use Chhaya to manipulate the homeowner. He can't wield her as a weapon against me.

She isn't mine to protect.

When night falls and the homeowner should be sleeping, the stairs creak. Someone searches for me in the cover of shadows.

I gather my thorned vines, preparing for a confrontation.

But the person who enters my room is Chhaya.

My plants writhe, frenzied and panicked. She mustn't be here. Not with me.

"I don't think you'll hurt me," she says, albeit hesitantly. She turns her face to the moonlight, a small welt on her cheek. "You couldn't even stand to scratch me."

The sight of the injury fills me with revulsion. I'm a demon. I always have been. Only something wicked would do that to a person.

I howl a gust of wind through the hallway, trying to coax her out of my room.

"Why won't you come near me?" Her expression, still illuminated, crumbles.

The image of the skull looms between us again, a warning to drive her away.

She doesn't retreat this time. Her hand reaches out. She touches me, my memory grasped in her palm. And the surrounding details fill in the rest of the picture. The clavicle bones and ribs. The tetul tree roots cradling the skeleton. Shiuli flowers sprouting from the remains.

"Oh," she breathes, "this is *you*."

The vision dissipates, but she won't let me go.

"Tell me how it happened."

She talks to me like there's humanity somewhere inside these walls. As if my monstrosity isn't the entire story. I can't tell her what she wants to know without curdling the way she looks at me, without revealing the terrible truth about myself that has evoked the homeowner's scorn for decades.

But if I don't show her, she'll keep coming back.

I could do it. Keep her with me for as long as we'd have. Let her be ruined by her husband in order to preserve myself in her eyes while she lives. After all, I'm depraved.

Chhaya's eyes glitter in the silver light.

The fog around us thickens. I sink into my past. And she, still watching my thoughts, comes with me.

I'm in the same room. My room. My father stands with me beside the window and tells me this house will be mine one day. I ask him if that's a promise, so he names it after me to prove it: Shiuli House.

Then I'm just over twenty, and he arranges my marriage. He secured me a good match, he tells me, because of the dowry he offered in exchange. I ask him what it is. Shiuli House, he answers.

The house that was meant to be mine. It is as mine as can be, he insists, since I will go with my husband.

My parents leave, and my bridegroom brings me back to my own home like I'm his guest.

I'm not the sole woman he invites into the house. There's the tall one married to the town doctor, and the milkman's daughter with the rosy cheeks. My favourite is the lady who goes from door to door selling flowers. She always saves me a shiuli, free of charge, because she likes my name. It's not the only thing she likes about me.

My husband catches us kissing. He tries to hit her, because she's his special friend and I'm his bride, but I throw myself at him. She runs because she's afraid. He strikes me instead, telling me I'm dangerous and disgusting and that he must punish me to protect the flower girl from my corruption.

I don't believe him, at first. I scream in protest. But when the neighbours don't stop him, and my father scolds me for disobeying him, the truth begins to seep in.

I must be evil, if this is the treatment they collectively condemn me to. They can't all be wrong about me.

He punishes me until there's more blood outside of me than in. He cleans himself in our bathroom, scarlet water pouring down the drain and to the flowers I planted outside in the garden. He buries my body, because arranging a public cremation would raise awkward conversations in the village.

The house that should have belonged to me in life, and that I belong to in death, preserves my memory.

When he leaves for the city, nobody stops him.

Because I was the monster. And everyone agrees I made him vanquish me.

"I told you to leave my wife alone."

Chhaya whirls around to face her husband. I'm too spent from revealing the very worst of myself to prevent his approach. He stands in the corridor, lit by the sunrise.

Her expression shutters, and she moves toward him. I want to put myself between them, to hurl myself at him before he lays a wretched hand on her.

Before I can react, she says, "I know the truth."

His mouth thins. "Do you?"

She nods. "The thing in this house, it wants to corrupt me. But you'll protect me from it."

Her censure scorches through to the depths of my being. I have to look away. Even after all these years, shame still makes a monster out of me.

The homeowner studies her. "Then you'll be pleased to know I found somebody to sell this property to. We can leave. Start over."

She bites her lip. "Aren't they all too afraid to come here?"

"They won't be, after I've burned the house down. The farmer along the road is willing to expand to this land if we remove everything on it." He turns to the darkness. Toward me. "*It gave me the idea.*"

"Oh." Chhaya nods slowly. "Yes, I think that's for the best. A deep cleanse to rid this place of its sinful creatures."

Her husband relaxes. "Pack your things. The farmer comes today."

I could chase her down the stairs with my vines, rattle the doors and windows to force her to listen to my pain until I'm nothing but a pile of ash—for even my stubborn memories cannot withstand a cremation.

But if also Chhaya, after seeing all of me, believes me a demon—then I should just let her slay me.

They prepare logs for when the farmer arrives. Together, they'll set me ablaze, and the farmer may rest easy knowing the conflagration will have chased out any lingering evil spirits.

Once the necessary arrangements have been made, Chhaya brews her husband his cha. She's the perfect bride I never was. She combs his hair with coconut oil. Smooths shaving cream over his jaw.

"I'm glad I know the truth," she tells him as she grooms his beard.

"Yes," he agrees. "Justice will be served at last."

"Indeed," she says, and digs the razor into his neck.

The house thrums as its owner splutters.

Chhaya takes a step back and watches her husband collapse to the ground. With this vanquishing, she carves me a new narrative, deep into his pliable flesh. Blood gushes out of his throat, and the uneven tiles beneath him drink thirstily. Her affection imbues my limbs with soft relief, with overwhelming tenderness. I feel almost shy, like a newlywed on the first night.

"Help me, Shiuli," she says.

My trembling vines drag his corpse outside. The pile of logs welcomes him, a deathbed waiting to ignite into his funeral pyre.

When the farmer arrives, Chhaya informs him of her husband's unfortunate shaving accident. "His hand slipped." Her voice quivers, though her eyes remain dry. "It was *awful*."

The farmer faces her downcast countenance and tuts sympathetically. "Do you still want to sell the land?" He glances around the haunted house nervously.

"Me? I'm not the owner."

"You're his widow. The house belongs to you now."

A muscle in her jaw twitches. "Then I shall stay a while. I, too, belong to it."

The farmer, still perched safely outside the gates, gives the building another uneasy look. "You want to live here by yourself, madam? That doesn't seem safe."

"No need to worry." Her fingers brush the blackened flowers growing in the yard. "I won't be by myself."

HE IS SURVIVED
BY HIS WIFE

JACKIE HEDEMAN

IN 2019, I WAS asked to write my own obituary. I was taking a professional development course for artists. The course was very goal-oriented (one year, five years, ten). Writing an obituary was another kind of long-term weather forecast. It was a version of the exercise screenwriter Angus Fletcher recommends: write the end so you know what you're aiming for.

I loved the assignment, but I struggled to complete it, in part because at that time in my life the things I wanted to imagine for myself felt so intangible (to be comfortable, to be married, to be remembered). There was a breathlessness to the obituary I wound up writing. It was a story I hadn't quite worked out how to tell, and the finished product was an attempt to prove something, if only to myself. It embarrassed me, reading it aloud to my cohort. How dare I want.

These days, my college roommates, Janie and CinCin, exist as squares on a screen. Many years past our final Princeton dorm room with its industrial carpet, we reunite monthly on Zoom.

Waiting to log in and greet them, I take stock of everything that's happened in the past month. New job. Taxes. Tearing down the shed with my neighbor; swinging a sledgehammer.

At some point, years ago, when I was first coming out to people, I lost track of who I'd told. I kept a list in my phone at first, but it was unreliable. There were people who knew without my telling them. There were people I was sure I'd told (there they were, on the list), who seemed surprised when I finally made a wide-release Facebook post.

With my closest friends scattered across the country, across the world, I still have trouble remembering who knows what about my life. "I may have already told you this," is a regular fall-back in most of my conversations, especially with the friends I mostly see on video calls. Did I ever tell Janie and CinCin about the brief span of months at the end of 2017, into 2018, when I long-distance dated my friend and writing partner, Molly? I can't remember the answer to this question when Molly and I start dating again, more seriously, in 2023.

It's a life update like any other, but the words lodge in my throat. Janie and CinCin know I'm queer, but for a long time they don't know that this queerness encompasses both bisexual-ity and asexuality, and in order to tell them this story, I must first own up to the years of not knowing myself as well as I wanted to. I have to begin to explain how that not-knowing kept me frozen. (Asexuality: how, for me?) In 2023, even though I have only just started to understand it all, I want to tell Janie and CinCin the full story. I need to. Within me, I feel a thaw.

When I was writing my obituary assignment, I returned to a fav-orite publication for inspiration. The *Princeton Alumni Weekly*'s

Memorials section unfurls in skinny, somber columns toward the end of each issue, sandwiched between Class Notes (babies and weddings) and the Classifieds (apartments in Provence and quasi-eugenicist matchmakers promising to find mature, educated women for you). Throughout the pages of the *PAW*, all history happens in jump cuts. ("University Won't Rename Wilson School or Wilson College," reads one April 2016 headline. "Citing Racism, Trustees Rethink Wilson and Rename Policy School," appears in September 2020. Neither of these headlines would exist if it weren't for the 33-hour sit-in led by the Black Justice League student group in 2015.)

The memorials, like all obituaries, fascinate me. What to emphasize, from an entire, sprawling life? In the *PAW* Memorials section, individuals are distilled down to their greatest accomplishments. This one invented a new form of cancer detection. This one became a Broadway mainstay. This one served in the army for decades. This one loved every grandchild. This one held public office. Chauffeured Albert Einstein. Joined the clergy. Founded a Fortune 500 company. He is survived by his wife.

Janie likes the Memorials that embrace life's humor. After she reads an entry for a recent grad, she makes CinCin and I promise to write each other's Memorials, to write hers. Maybe throw in the part about the freshman year phlegm spittoon or the senior year tarot reader. Obviously, we agree immediately. What grief it would be, to see my friends boiled down to accomplishments. I want them weird and beautiful, in full color. I want anyone reading their obituaries to feel that somewhere, around a corner, they are still alive.

When Molly and I dated the first time, I was so anxious I couldn't eat. I drove the seven hours to visit her chewing on stick after stick of wintergreen Extra. I nearly shat myself, barely making it to the first Kum & Go over the Minnesota state line. The source of all this tumult was a very prosaic thing: I'd never dated before and I didn't know what I was supposed to do. I wanted to be with her, but when I was with her, I was gripped with fear.

I didn't know what was wrong with me. I spent the following years cold, searching for words to explain myself—to explain when and why that prey feeling strikes, to explain that it doesn't always. When we got back together years later, I lived with the memory of the fear but also with the freeing knowledge that my queerness was a mansion, with rooms upon rooms of feeling. Desire lived in some of those rooms. In some rooms, love, community, history, favorite characters, certain shoes, legacy.

Molly was in those rooms. I knew that we belonged together, but in what way? For the first five months of our renewed relationship, I didn't know what to call her. I already knew that "writing partner" wasn't big enough. Over the years, I'd stretched it to capacity, trying to signal that Molly was unique in my life, so important, someone I would never move on from. Our writing lived in the rooms, every word, but she was more to me than our writing.

Flip straight to the Memorials section and scan the last paragraph of each entry. He is survived by his wife. Next entry. He is survived by his wife. Next entry. His wife of fifty years survives him. Next entry. He is survived by his wife.

I remember a man from one of those older classes. I interviewed him for the final paper for a class on the history of sexuality. I spoke with him on Skype for hours about being gay (he preferred "homosexual") at Princeton, though he clearly wanted to talk about other things: racial bigotry at the Eating Clubs, nights playing in the band, the fact that for a long time he didn't want to be part of the alumni community, as though any of us have any choice in the matter. The *PAW* knows where to find us.

As we talked, a toddler wandered into frame. "My grandson," my interviewee said. "My wife's out getting lunch."

"Oh," I said. It was 2010. I was twenty-one. "You..." I couldn't find the words.

He smiled at me across all that distance: him in his desk chair, me on my dorm room floor. He is survived by his wife.

What have I been looking for, all these years?

He is survived by his brother, sister, nieces and nephews. He is remembered as a kind and witty friend. He will be missed by the Episcopalian church choir where he devoted so much energy. Turn the page again. More recent classes leave the truth unvarnished. He is survived by his partner of twenty years. He is survived by his husband of six years.

I am heartened by this shift, but I miss the aunts, uncles, choir members. I comb the Memorials section for them. What proof do we need that someone was queer? What proof do I need? In my twenties, I searched everywhere to find the exact word for my yearning. In the Memorials section, I just want to see proof of life.

The way I felt about Molly didn't have to be succinct, but— beautiful problem—it had to be legible. The first time we were together, very few people knew. Now, I wanted to tell everyone.

I took months to mull it over. Spring became summer became fall. I climbed through thin mountain air and thought of her. I attended a friend's memorial and thought of her. Walking on the beach in North Carolina before my cousin's wedding, headphones left behind at the Airbnb, I couldn't *stop* thinking about her. I took a picture of the water and sent it to her. On a stretch of unoccupied sand, I drew our initials with my finger. I laughed at myself while I did it—what the fuck?—but I did it all the same. I imagined her there with me. I thought about the way she inches me closer to myself. There was a dizzy joy in my stomach. These were girlfriend feelings, I decided. These were love feelings.

I tell Janie and CinCin about years-worth of weekly Skype chats, about the title "writing partner" bursting at the seams with meaning, about the way my heart fizzed like seafoam. They listen quietly. At the end, CinCin stares at me. "And, sorry, *why* would you not be calling her your girlfriend?"

I assumed that once I finally found myself in a relationship with someone, I would know the steps to a dance that's been danced since the beginning of time. My lips would find theirs. Desire would swing through my body like Miley Cyrus straddling a wrecking ball. And if I couldn't name the steps, couldn't hum the tune, they would. That's the way it went in everything I read.

I couldn't predict it would be more like this: years of friendship (naturally occurring), then months of dating (breathless), then friendship (white-knuckled), friendship (hard-won), friendship (unlike any other), then a walk on a beach and a warm, sudden realization. For us, there is no choreography. I call her my girlfriend because she already is.

I think, in the end, it should go something like this: Jackie Hedeman lived a long, full life. She traveled again and again to the
places and people she loved best. She learned herself over and
over. She wrote constantly and laughed a lot. She loved Dippin'
Dots more than was strictly justified. Once, on her birthday, her
dentist hand-delivered a bottle of red wine. Once, in high school,
a classmate called her handwriting "masculine and neurotic."
She was a light sleeper. She knew exactly when to arrive at the air-
port and exactly when to leave a party. She left her corner of the
world better than she found it. She is survived by her wife.

CONTRIBUTORS

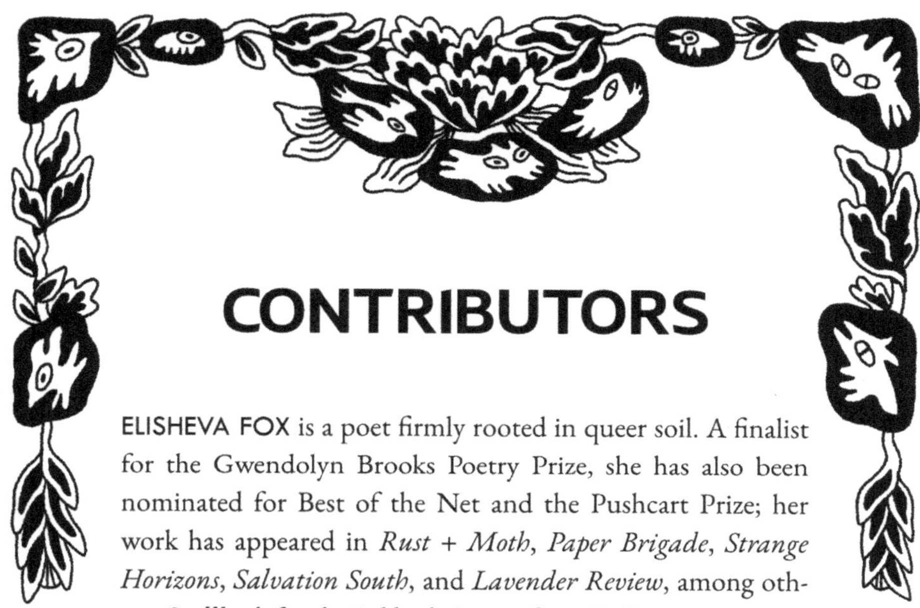

ELISHEVA FOX is a poet firmly rooted in queer soil. A finalist for the Gwendolyn Brooks Poetry Prize, she has also been nominated for Best of the Net and the Pushcart Prize; her work has appeared in *Rust + Moth*, *Paper Brigade*, *Strange Horizons*, *Salvation South*, and *Lavender Review*, among others. *Spellbook for the Sabbath Queen*, from Belle Point Press, is her first collection of poems, and was selected for Jewish Women's Archive 2023-2024 Book Club Picks.

ELENA SICHROVSKY (she/they/it) is a queer disabled author and cult survivor. They enjoy deep sea creatures, body horror, and Don Hertzfeldt films. Their debut poetry chapbook *Eating Out Anne Sexton* is free to download from Ghost City Press. You can read more stories on its website, www.elenasichrovsky.com, or find them on Bluesky @esichr.bsky.social or Instagram @elenitasich.

SIMO SRINIVAS writes about all things weird and queer. Their short stories have appeared in several speculative fiction magazines and anthologies, including *Fantasy Magazine*, *Strange Horizons*, *khōréō*, and *Archive of the Odd*, among others. Simo was a 2025 Lambda Literary Fellow and Tenebrous Press' Brave New Weird Breakout Author of 2023. When not writing, they can be found on the trail scoping out the ruins of old mining towns and counting pikas. You can also find them online at www.srinivassimo.com.

ANN LEBLANC is a writer, editor, and woodworker. Her debut novella, *THE TRANSITIVE PROPERTIES OF CHEESE*, is a cyberpunk cheese-heist, published by Neon Hemlock. Ann is the editor of *EMBODIED EXEGESIS*, an anthology of cyberpunk and posthuman stories by transfem authors. Her short fiction has been published in *Strange Horizons, Clarkesworld Magazine, Escape Pod*, and *Baffling Magazine*. You can find her in cyberspace at www.annleblanc.com.

ISHMAEL GREY is a damp, drizzly November soul who wants to hear your whale facts. He occasionally emerges from a cave to visit the library or attend metal concerts. He went to the Viable Paradise writing workshop in 2022. This is his first publication. Find him online at www.ishmaelgrey.com.

TANADRIN's natural habitat is library stacks and the backs of used bookstores. She grew up in Nashville, spent a decade in Dublin, and now lives in Berlin with her wife and a very fluffy cat. She is interested in historical linguistics, space travel, and deep time. She can be found online at www.tanadrin.de and @tanadrin.bsky.social.

RICK HOLLON is a genderqueer writer, parent, cat mom, and photographer living in Upstate New York. Their poems have appeared or are forthcoming in *Kaleidotrope, Analog, ALOCASIA, Delicate Friend*, and elsewhere. Their first full-length poetry collection, *Time Travel Is Easy*, was published in 2025. A second collection, *Prayers to the Summer Queen*, will come out later this year. Find them and their writings at www.mimulus.weebly.com.

ABIGAIL ELIZA (she/they) really likes swords, and queer medieval poetry, and contra dance, and her friends. They write the

Audio Verse Award-winning audio drama *Back Again, Back Again*, a story about alternate realms, ex-prophecy children, and queer girls with swords. Her work has been published in *Folklore Review, Stone Circle, Stone of Madness*, Washington State's Queer Poetry Anthology, and elsewhere. Ideally, right now, they are in the woods. On the internet, you can find out more about them at www.abigailelizawrites.carrd.co.

SARAH PAULING is a higher education professional in Seattle. A graduate of the Viable Paradise workshop, her stories have appeared in places like *Clarkesworld, Strange Horizons*, and *Escape Pod*. In her spare time, she sings barbershop harmony and reads comics in order to complain about them. Find her on Bluesky @sarahpauling.

CYPHER (she/her) is a self-taught brown and queer Tamizh diaspora poet living in Canada. Her writing is deeply musical, political, philosophical, and introspective. Her work has been featured by the *Dark Winter Literary Magazine, Arcana Poetry Press, FeelsZine*, and several other publications. You can find Cypher on Instagram @cypherspace_101.

NADIA RADOVICH is an author based in Washington, D.C., with work in *Apex, Strange Horizons, Flash Fiction Online*, and others. You can find Nadia on Bluesky @nadiaradovich.bsky.social or at www.nadiaradovich.com.

SEOUNG KIM is a Koream librarian who lives on the lands of the Council of the Three Fires near Chicago. He has work in *Lightspeed Magazine, Fantasy Magazine*, and elsewhere.

NICO SANTANA is a Filipino poet from Quezon City whose poetry has been published in *The Broadkill Review*, *Bluestem Magazine*, and *TLDTD*, among others. Aside from poetry, he likes to write scripts and storyboards for comics and video games he never plans to actually make.

AYIDA SHONIBAR (she/they) writes dark and wistful speculative fiction about misfits, monsters, mischief-makers. A Lambda Literary Fellow and previous We Need Diverse Books mentee, they have also received support from the Horror Writers Association, Dream Foundry, and Grub Street for their work. Spanning genres and age categories, their short stories, essays, and poetry appear in various publications, including *Apex Magazine*, *Baffling Magazine*, *Silk & Sinew* (Bad Hand Books), *Heartlines Spec*, *Nature Futures*, *Night of the Living Queers* (Wednesday Books), and *Transmogrify!* (Harper Teen), among others. You can find more information at www.ayidashonibar.com.

JACKIE HEDEMAN is a queer Midwesterner. Her work has appeared in *Foglifter*, *Fugue*, *Electric Literature*, *The Offing*, and elsewhere. With Molly Olguín, she is the co-creator of *The Pasithea Powder*, a queer, sci-fi audio drama. Find her at www.jacquelinhedeman.com.

COVER ARTIST

THEO MARCIAL's mind is a densely-packed library of biographical accounts of people who have and have not existed. They'll draw and even write things for you, so long as you don't mind all the portraits keeping them company. They can be found interring and exhuming their stories on the nearest sunny porch, trawling eBay for vintage ephemera, or haunting mediums print and digital under the epithet they stole from Hannibal Barca. They owe everything they are as an artist to Latin poetry and

Oshima Nagisa's *IN THE REALM OF THE SENSES* (1976). Find them at www.hvmator.com.

INTERIOR ARTIST

RIS (they/them) is a non-binary designer and illustrator. They draw influence from traditional animation, Asian historical painting and statues, as well as the organic and the natural world. They are inspired by art and storytelling as a way to communicate our values and history and create community connections, and also because it's fun to draw cute creatures. Their work can be found at www.imaginarybeasts.net or over on Instagram as @demonography.

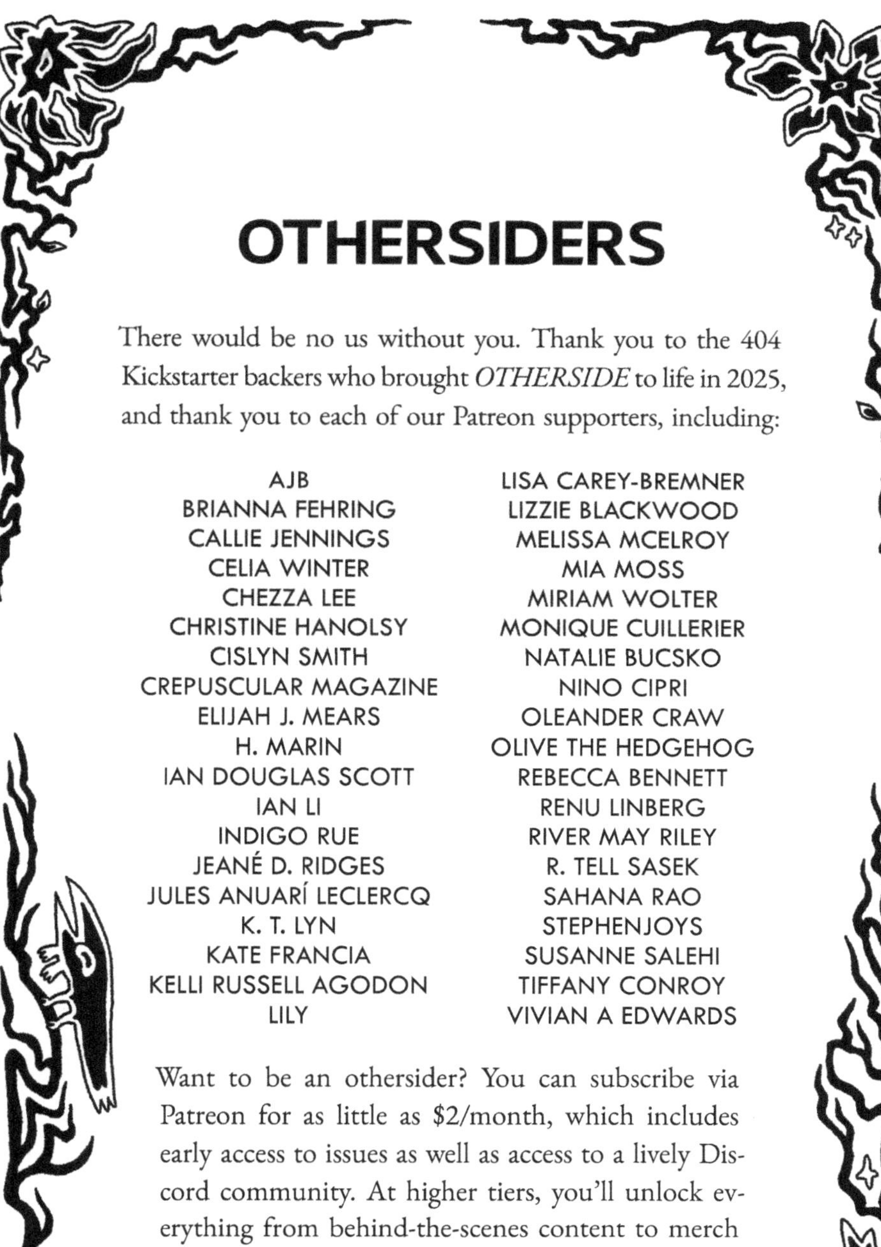

OTHERSIDERS

There would be no us without you. Thank you to the 404 Kickstarter backers who brought *OTHERSIDE* to life in 2025, and thank you to each of our Patreon supporters, including:

AJB
BRIANNA FEHRING
CALLIE JENNINGS
CELIA WINTER
CHEZZA LEE
CHRISTINE HANOLSY
CISLYN SMITH
CREPUSCULAR MAGAZINE
ELIJAH J. MEARS
H. MARIN
IAN DOUGLAS SCOTT
IAN LI
INDIGO RUE
JEANÉ D. RIDGES
JULES ANUARÍ LECLERCQ
K. T. LYN
KATE FRANCIA
KELLI RUSSELL AGODON
LILY

LISA CAREY-BREMNER
LIZZIE BLACKWOOD
MELISSA MCELROY
MIA MOSS
MIRIAM WOLTER
MONIQUE CUILLERIER
NATALIE BUCSKO
NINO CIPRI
OLEANDER CRAW
OLIVE THE HEDGEHOG
REBECCA BENNETT
RENU LINBERG
RIVER MAY RILEY
R. TELL SASEK
SAHANA RAO
STEPHENJOYS
SUSANNE SALEHI
TIFFANY CONROY
VIVIAN A EDWARDS

Want to be an othersider? You can subscribe via Patreon for as little as $2/month, which includes early access to issues as well as access to a lively Discord community. At higher tiers, you'll unlock everything from behind-the-scenes content to merch discounts to print subscriptions. Every dollar raised via Patreon goes directly to author and artist pay, always. Join us! We hope to see you on the otherside!

ABOUT *OTHERSIDE*

OTHERSIDE is a queer-led literary magazine that publishes speculative fiction, poetry, nonfiction, and art by 2SLGBTQIA+ creators. Inspired by José Esteban Muñoz's definition of queerness as "an insistence on potentiality or concrete possibility for another world," we reject the present. Instead, we dream of a future we call the otherside: a future defined by possibility, a future in which marginalized authors and artists are no longer confined to the margins. We believe that queer stories by queer authors matter, now more than ever.

We publish quarterly issues in March, June, September, and December. Each issue contains at least 16,000 words of original fiction and poetry plus original art, reprints, and nonfiction, all by authors and artists who self-identify as 2SLGBTQIA+. We believe in making great literature accessible, and each issue is freely available online; subscribers get early access. You can subscribe via Patreon for as little as $2/month at **www.patreon.com/othersidespec** or learn more about other ways to support us on our website, **www.othersidespec.com**.

Want to make sure you never miss an issue? Our Patreon has a free tier with a monthly newsletter. You can also follow us on Bluesky, Instagram, Tumblr, TikTok, and elsewhere at the handle @othersidespec. (We're everywhere, but we are most active on Bluesky and Instagram!)

OTHERSIDE is published by Hybris Press, a 501(c)(3) nonprofit organization devoted to sharing and promoting queer art. In an increasingly hostile world, Hybris Press and *OTHERSIDE* only exist thanks to your support, including subscriptions and donations. Thank you for reading, following along, leaving reviews, and telling your friends about the work we publish. We couldn't do any of this without you.